£4.95

THIS'LL KILL YA

And other dangerous stories

by Harry Willson

CAUTION! PROCEED AT YOUR OWN RISK.

III Publishing
P.O. Box 170363
San Francisco, CA 94117-0363

1st Printing: January, 1991

Illustrations by Claiborne O'Connor
Cover by Bill Meyers

Copyright © 1991 by Harry Willson

All rights reserved.

THIS'LL KILL YA was performed as a play at the Vortex Theatre, in Albuquerque, New Mexico, in February, 1981. Contact the publisher directly about royalty arrangements

Contents

THIS'LL KILL YA
(THE LAST WORD ON CENSORSHIP)   5

ACTS OF GOD   109

SOLILOQUY
WITH FIVE INTERRUPTIONS   135

SABOTAGE   179

CAUTION! READING THIS
BOOK MAY BE HAZARDOUS
TO YOUR HEALTH!

THIS'LL KILL YA

(THE LAST WORD ON CENSORSHIP)

One

Detective Keith Bright entered his dull-grey office and removed his wet see-through plastic raincoat. He stepped past the large cluttered desk and hung the dripping raincoat on an old-fashioned wooden coat rack in the corner. He took off his black suit jacket and draped it on the chair behind his desk. While he stared unseeing out the dirty casement window, he loosened his black tie.

He stepped to the large metal bookcase beyond the filing cabinets and fingered some manila folders. He moved to the desk and turned on the radio. Again he stepped to the window and stared out, hands clasped behind him.

The radio announcer's voice filled the dingy office. "... funeral of Mr. Titus Cramp, held today at Providence Church in this city, with the Reverend Kent Boyer officiating. Mr. Cramp was an experienced and highly respected police detective who worked thirty years for this city's law enforcement department. He was unmarried, and dedicated all his time to his work and his church. Now turning to the weather --"

Keith sat behind the desk. "Rain has continued throughout the night and early morning. Clearing is expected by late afternoon, with a high temperature --" The detective snapped off the radio.

His secretary, Tracey Ellsworth, strode in from the outer office. "Here's that autopsy you wanted. Came this morning." She handed him a manila folder, and brushed imaginary lint from the front of her stylish dark blue uniform.

"What's it say?" Keith asked as he took the folder.

"Not much. Heart stopped. No reason why."

Keith glanced at the paper without really reading it. "Not poison?" he asked.

"Nope."

Keith stood up. "I can't understand it. A perfectly good man, sitting at his desk, doing his job -- drops dead. Not a mark on him. Nothing wrong with him. What could have happened?" He stopped and pondered, and shook his head. "To think that Titus is gone. And we don't know why."

"Why?" Tracey looked at the ceiling, thinking hard. "Why did Titus die? Deep question. Why does anyone die?"

"Stop that," Keith said flatly. "No philosophy games. I mean what caused it?"

"We don't know," Tracey said, somewhat philosophically. A side door opened suddenly and Police Chief Maureen Kelly stalked in. Tracey looked sharp and exclaimed, "Good morning, Chief!"

"Good morning." Chief Kelly's voice was tense, and she appeared to be under severe strain.

"Chief, you look awful," Tracey said with concern.

"Damn rain," she muttered in reply.

Tracey started toward her door to the outer office. "Yeah, the rain just adds to the misery."

Chief Kelly addressed Keith. "Here's your next assignment." She held up a manila folder. Tracey paused at her door, curious.

"So soon after the funeral?" Keith asked. "But, then, why not?" He smiled wanly. "May as well work as sit around and feel bad doing nothing."

"Nobody sits around here doing nothing," growled Chief Kelly. She handed Keith the folder.

"You're right. And you're the chief." Keith said, taking the folder. "Anything interesting?"

"It could be your most important case," the chief said.

Tracey stepped toward Keith, very much interested. "Oh, something big, huh?"

Keith was more casual. "What's up?" he asked the chief.

"Read that and find out," she told him. "And keep it quiet." To Tracey she added, "No reporters, no leaks, no nothing." She turned back to Keith. "That's what Titus was working on. His last case." Keith opened the folder. "If it IS a case," she added.

"What does THAT mean?" Keith asked. He fingered the papers in the open folder. "Not much here." He lay the folder open on his desk and flipped papers. "Newspaper clippings. Obits. And this." He picked up a paperback book with a clean white cover. "What's this?"

"That's a book," the chief said testily. "Titus was reading it at his desk. It's part of that file."

"It explains the clippings, maybe? And these obits?"

"Maybe," growled the chief. "You find out." She started toward her door. "That's your assignment."

"I'll get to my desk," said Tracey. She went out and closed the door after her.

Keith was riffling through the book as Chief Kelly passed through the door to her inner office. "Hey, Chief!" he exclaimed.

She wheeled back into his office. "What?"

"The last pages here are stapled shut."

"That's right," she said. "Leave 'em that way."

Keith opened the book nearer the front and read a little. "Hey, what IS this stuff?"

"You read it. Carefully," she added.

Keith read aloud. "THE GUILT PAGES." He held the book closer to his face in order to read fine print. "CAUTION! IF YOU BELIEVE THAT TAKING THE BLAME AND WALLOWING IN THOUGHTS OF GUILT

ARE BAD, READING THESE PAGES MAY BE HAZARDOUS TO YOUR HEALTH." He looked up at Chief Kelly. "What is this?"

He held the book at a normal distance from his face and continued reading. "I BROKE THE LAMP."

He ran a finger down the page, reading each line slowly, as if reciting a poem.

"I PEED MY PANTS.

"I LIED ABOUT THAT. AND THAT.

"I TOUCHED HER BREASTS, AND IT WAS NO ACCIDENT.

"I TOUCHED HIS CROTCH AND HE GOT A HARD-ON." Keith looked up. "Chief, what the hell IS this?"

"It's a book. Read it."

"I never saw such stuff." He turned several pages and continued reading. "THE GUILT PAGES CONTINUED.

"I SEDUCED THE MAILMAN.

"I CHEATED ON MY INCOME TAX.

"THERE IS NOTHING SECRET THAT SHALL NOT BE MADE KNOWN." He looked up again. "Stupid crap. Why is this in Titus' file?" He turned the page and read more.

"I SPENT THE NIGHT IN A WHORE HOUSE."

"Really?" asked the Chief.

Keith shook the book and glared at her. "I'm reading this crap!" He looked down and continued.

"I HIT MY KID, AND IT WAS A BEATING, NOT A SPANKING.

"I VOTED FOR A LIAR, AND THEN A CROOK."

He closed the book. "Look, Chief --"

"I don't mean for you to stand there and read the book to me," the chief stated. She pointed at his chest. "I mean YOU read it. And get to the bottom of it." She turned away and went into her office, closing the door behind her.

Keith read silently for a little. Tracey opened her door quietly and came in. Keith jerked, as if guilty, and slammed the book shut. Then he grinned sheepishly at Tracey. "Listen to this damn book, Trace." He opened it again. "I never saw the like." Tracey sat and Keith began reading.

"THE VIOLENCE PAGES." He held the book close again for fine print. "CAUTION! IF YOU BELIEVE THAT THINKING VIOLENT THOUGHTS IS DANGEROUS OR INJURIOUS, READING THESE PAGES MAY BE HAZARDOUS TO YOUR HEALTH." He held the book at a normal distance. "I CATCH A GRASSHOPPER AND PULL OFF ONE WING AT A TIME, THEN ONE LEG AT A TIME, THEN I PULL THE BELLY-PART OFF, AND THEN THE HEAD."

Tracey made a face. "Yuk. That's terrible."

Keith continued reading. "I PUNCH MY FATHER IN THE MOUTH, KNOCK HIM

DOWN, KICK HIM IN THE BELLY AND THEN IN THE HEAD, AND THEN CUT OFF HIS TESTICLES." Keith licked his lips. "God Almighty."

Tracey raised her hands and pursed her lips in disgust. "That's horrible."

Keith read on:

> I CATCH A ROBBER IN MY HOUSE. I TIE HIM UP AND PULL OUT HIS TOENAILS AND FINGERNAILS WITH PLIERS, RUN A HOSE UP HIS ANUS AND TURN ON THE WATER. WHEN HE OPENS HIS MOUTH TO SCREAM, I CUT OFF HIS TONGUE WITH TIN SHEARS.

"Jesus Christ!" exclaimed Tracey.

Keith looked up. "Ah, yes. The Inquisition." He turned the page. "Let me read some more."

> I AM OPERATING A MACHINE GUN IN A BATTLE AT THE EDGE OF A BIG FIELD. I TURN THE GUN ON A LINE OF MEN AS THEY COME OUT OF THE WOODS AND DOWN A DIRT BANK. I HIT THEM IN THE CHEST, IN THE HEAD, IN THE BELLY. THEY FALL AND BEGIN TO PILE UP ON THE BANK. THE BODIES SQUIRM. MORE MEN KEEP

> COMING OUT OF THE WOODS AND I KEEP MOWING THEM DOWN.

Tracey held her stomach. "That's sick."

"That's war," Keith muttered. He flipped the page and read more.

> I TIE HER ON THE BED, ONE WRIST TO EACH HEAD-POST AND ONE ANKLE TO EACH FOOT-POST. SHE IS NAKED. SEE ALSO THE SEX PAGES. I STRIKE HER WITH A SMALL LEATHER WHIP, ON THE LEGS, ON THE ARMS, IN HER UNDERARMS, ON THE INSIDE OF HER THIGHS. I TOSS LITTLE NEEDLE-POINT DARTS AT HER BREASTS AND BELLY. I TAKE OUT A SHARP KNIFE AND --

Tracey stood and interrupted the reading. "For God's sake, stop that!"

Keith looked up at Tracey, a little pale in the face. "Gets to ya, doesn't it?" He turned the book over, holding his place, and looked at the plain white cover.

"Where the hell did that come from?" Tracey asked.

"That's what I gotta find out," Keith said. "I guess." He turned a few more pages and read again.

"THE VIOLENCE PAGES CONTINUED."
He looked up. "It's like a poem."

"Some poem," growled Tracey.

"No, I mean the way the page is printed."

Tracey curled her lip. "Read the damn thing."

Keith read:

> I HATE, AND AM READY TO MAIM
> AND KILL, ALL JEWS.
> I HATE, AND AM READY TO MAIM
> AND KILL, ALL CATHOLICS.
> I HATE, AND AM READY TO MAIM
> AND KILL, ALL PROTESTANTS.

Tracey interrupted. "Well, he gets 'em all."

"Yep." Keith ran his finger down the right hand margin.

> -- ALL NIGGERS.
> -- ALL CHINKS.
> -- ALL SPICKS.
> -- ALL HONKIES.
> -- ALL MICKS.
> -- ALL ARABS.

Hmmm. Hmmm. Hmmm.

> I HATE, AND AM READY TO MAIM
> AND KILL, ALL CHILDREN.

Tracey interrupted again. "Oh, that's awful."

"Take it easy," said Keith. "It's just a book. A stupid, sick book." He read further.

"I HATE, AND AM READY TO MAIM AND KILL, ALL WHALES."

He ran his finger down the margin again.

"-- ALL SEALS.
-- ALL PANDA BEARS.
-- ALL ELEPHANTS.
-- ALL LIONS.
-- ALL TREES."

He looked up at Tracey again. "Get his last line --

"I HATE, AND AM READY TO MAIM AND KILL, ALL LIVING THINGS." He closed the book. "This person is seriously ill."

"What person?" Tracey asked.

Keith glared at the cover of the book. "The author of this stuff."

"What else is in the file?"

"Good question," said Keith, laying the book down. "Let's see." He picked up a newspaper clipping from the folder. He dropped it and picked up another. "Obit clippings. A woman in her living room. Unexpectedly." He dropped the clipping and picked up another. "A woman on the bus. Unexpectedly. Autopsy inconclusive. Church funeral. Pall-bearers." He looked up at Tracey. "Why is Titus collecting obits?"

"Beats me," Tracey admitted. "Are they related? To each other, I mean."

Keith spread out several clippings on his desk. "Let's see." He studied for a moment. "Well, now, here's a husband and wife. Both unexpected. A week apart. And here's a Mrs. Flandermeyer --" He began flipping through loose yellow legal sheets. "What was Titus up to?" He read from the sheets. "'Mrs. Flandermeyer -- on the bus. Mr. Manling -- at home in bed. Mrs. Manling -- at home in her living room. Hypothesis --'" Keith looked up. "Here we go. Titus's hypothesis." He read carefully.

"'Each victim died after reading the book. Mrs. Flandermeyer died on the bus. Mr. Manling, the bus driver, took the book home, after the ambulance attendants left it, behind the seat, or someplace. He died in his bed, reading the book. His wife, a week later, still in possession of the book, died in her reading chair in her living room. I now have possession of the book in question.'" Keith stared into Tracey's face. "What kind of silliness is this?"

"I'm sure I don't know," whispered Tracey.

The door to the inner office opened and Chief Kelly entered. Keith stared into Tracey's face and continued. "I can't believe Titus could be serious."

"About what?" barked the chief.

"About this whole business, Chief. It's too crazy -- too stupid. If I understand Titus' notes, he thinks there's a connection between three unexpected and unexplained deaths."

"So?" said Chief Kelly, arching a black eyebrow. "Get to the bottom of it."

"And he thinks the connection is this book!" cried Keith.

"So?" Chief Kelly brushed her red hair back with her hand. "Check it out."

"Is he blaming those three deaths on a book?"

"It's a hypothesis. Every one of those persons, it appears, was reading that book." She gestured toward it as it lay on Keith's desk. "At the time of death. Autopsies aren't explaining anything."

"Three deaths, caused by a book."

"Four," corrected Chief Kelly.

"Four?" Keith scratched among the clippings and then suddenly jerked back. "Oh, my God! You mean Titus, too!"

"Evidently. Titus was reading that book at his desk at the time of death."

Keith became excited. "Well, run lab tests on the book, on the binding, on the glue in the binding, on the ink. On the staples in the back." He looked at his hands, and wiggled his fingers.

Chief Kelly was crisp and businesslike. "Titus was an old pro, Mr. Bright. He did that already. No chemicals. No poisons. No indication of poison in the autopsies, or in the lab analysis of the book. And don't worry about the staples."

"Why not?"

"Because I stapled it, just before I handed the file over to you."

"Whatever for?"

"I don't want you killed." Chief Kelly was deadly serious.

"Killed?" howled Keith. "How'm I gonna get killed if there's no poison?"

"I don't know. I know I need you on the case. If there IS a case. Danger is part of the job here, but I don't want you hurt needlessly or carelessly."

"Danger!" gasped Keith, staring in disbelief at his boss.

Tracey reached toward him. "Titus is dead, Keith. Take it easy, and pay attention."

He exerted force to calm himself down very deliberately. "O.K., O.K. Now lemme get this straight. Three -- no, FOUR people are dead. Titus thought this book --" Keith stalled. He picked up the book gingerly, and then looked at Chief Kelly. "You think --" He stopped and scratched his head. "You think the danger is in READING it?" The chief raised her shoulders and gestured "Who-knows?" with her hands. "Reading it," Keith continued. "Reading ALL of it. So you stapled the last pages shut." He paused. All three were silent a moment. "That's incredible," Keith said, finally. He waved the book just a little in his hand. "There's certainly been no effect on me so far," he said with a faint smile.

"Are you sure?" the Chief asked quietly.

Keith touched his chest, pulled his ear with his free hand, scratched his hair. "Sure. I feel fine. Fine."

Tracey fluffed her hair and rubbed her lower arms. "And hearing it didn't hurt me any," she said to Chief Kelly. "I don't think," she added.

Keith held up the book and read the cover. "THIS'LL KILL YA. THE LAST WORD ON CENSORSHIP." He held the book closer to his face, to read fine print on the cover. "CAUTION: READING THIS BOOK MAY BE HAZARDOUS TO YOUR HEALTH." He looked up again, glancing from Chief Kelly to Tracey. "A line swiped from the tobacco and liquor people."

"No, Keith. From the Surgeon General," Tracey corrected.

Keith opened the cover and read the title page. "THIS'LL KILL YA. CAUTION. PROCEED AT YOUR OWN RISK." Again he stopped and looked at the women. "Aw, c'mon. Is this some gag?"

"No, Mr. Bright. No gag." The Chief headed toward her door. "Four dead people. And the only clue is that book."

Keith waved the book after her. "You really think that this is the book, which, if you read it, it'll kill ya?"

"I don't know," the Chief admitted very soberly. "I think Titus believed that."

"Why'd he read it, then? Why'd he LET it kill him?"

"I don't know," the Chief said quietly. "I don't know whether it kills, or how. Your assignment is to clear this up. And don't get killed carrying it out."

Keith shook his head. "Thanks for the concern." He opened the book again, near the middle. "I just can't believe it. This is the book that, if ya read it, it'll kill ya. So read it, but don't let it kill ya. It's too crazy."

"Lots of deadly things are," the Chief stated ominously and went back into her inner office.

Two

Tracey sat in Keith's chair. He stared into her face a moment. "Let's hear some more of it," she suggested.

Keith turned pages without looking. "Damnedest thing," he muttered. "Read it, but be careful, 'cause if you read it, it'll kill ya." He looked down and read aloud. "THE MAGIC WORDS CONTINUED. THE MEAN FIGHTING WORDS." He moved the book and squinted for the fine print. "CAUTION! IF YOU BELIEVE THAT WORDS CAN BE USED AS WEAPONS TO HARM PERSONS, READING THESE PAGES MAY BE HAZARDOUS TO YOUR HEALTH. SEE ALSO THE FINDING OUT PAGES."

"What does that mean?" Tracey asked.

"I'm sure I don't know. Another section, maybe." He read some more. "YOU ARE A BASTARD. Says in parenthesis I should shout it." Keith yelled, "YOU ARE A BASTARD!!" He turned the page and read, "THE MAGIC WORDS CONTINUED." He paused, and then shouted, "YOU ARE A SON OF A BITCH!!" Tracey stared at him wide-eyed.

He continued in a normal tone of voice.

> IT MUST BE NOTED THAT IF THESE WORDS ARE AIMED AT A MALE, THEY MISS. IN BOTH CASES THEY HIT HIS MOTHER, WITH WHATEVER CONSEQUENCES. ONE SAYS SHE WASN'T MARRIED WHEN HE WAS CONCEIVED AND BORN. THE OTHER SAYS SHE IS A FEMALE DOG, PROBABLY MEANT METAPHORICALLY.

Tracey was very thoughtful. "Y'know, I've thought of that. Those words are pure male chauvinism."

Keith looked up at her. "Sounds like something Chief would say."

"Reminds me of her anti-rape campaign. Read some more."

Keith continued.

> IN THE SEARCH FOR EXPRESSIONS OF HOSTILITY AIMED AT MALES, WHICH DO NOT ALSO OR PRIMARILY INJURE FEMALES, THE ENGLISH LANGUAGE IS IN DIFFICULTY.

He shouted again. "YOU ARE A PRICK!!" He paused, then yelled, "YOU ARE A HORSE'S ASS!!" The two of them had to grin. Keith read on in a normal voice.

> THERE IS NOT MUCH MAGIC. ONE USES A PART OF THE ANATOMY TO REFER TO THE WHOLE. SEE THE FUNCTION WORDS. THE OTHER IS CLEARLY METAPHORICAL, REFERRING TO A PART OF THE ANATOMY OF A HORSE IN A MANNER WHICH IS FAR FROM CLEAR.

The police detective and his secretary were startled to hear a voice in the doorway to Tracey's office. "May we come in?" Tracey jumped up quickly. Keith closed the book, lay it on his desk and stood cautiously. The intruder was a middle-aged man, dressed in a black suit and clerical collar.

Tracey spoke. "Yes, come in. You must be Mr. Boyer."

"I am," the clergyman said. He offered his hand to Keith. "And you must be Mr. Bright." The two men shook hands. "I have an appointment with Police Chief Kelly."

"Oh, really?" said Keith. "You sure got the jump on us."

"That was my fault, Keith," said Tracey. "But he's O.K." To Mr. Boyer, she said, "I'll tell her you're here." She pressed the intercom button on Keith's desk.

Chief Kelly's voice came over the intercom. "Yes?"

"Mr. Boyer's here to see you, Chief."

"Very good. Send him in."

Mr. Boyer crossed to the inner door. "I'll just go on in through here," he stated, and went into Chief Kelly's office.

Tracey was staring at another newcomer who was blocking the door to the outer office. "You must be --" she began.

"I'm MRS. Boyer, Chairperson of the Mayor's Citizen's Censorship Committee," the woman announced in an extremely haughty tone. She was middle-aged, no longer good-looking, dressed in frumpy style, with a long-sleeved blouse closed tightly at the neck, half-long skirt, practical shoes, and a little old-fashioned hat of the type that women who hate hats used to wear to church. She stepped toward the door through which her husband had just disappeared, but Tracey was blocking her way. At that moment Chief Kelly reached in and grabbed the handle of her door and pulled it shut firmly. "Well!" exclaimed Mrs. Boyer. "Did you ever?"

"Ever what?" asked Keith.

"Ever see such --" But then Mrs. Boyer interrupted herself. "But, never mind. You ARE Mr. Bright, the police detective?" Keith nodded. "I came to see you anyway, not her."

"Me?" asked Keith, surprised.

"Yes. A suggestion. A request."

"What is it?"

"You know about the Mayor's Citizens' Censorship Committee, of which I am chairperson?" Mrs. Boyer pressed her hand against her ample chest.

"Vaguely," said Keith.

"Our committee previews films and does periodic checks on the filthy bookstores around town."

"Oh, yes," said Keith. "I've heard them referred to as 'Sunday School raids.'"

"Our opponents call them that. When we recommend that something is really too, too much, the mayor has the authority to forbid its sale, or public viewing."

"Oh." Keith's voice was flat.

Mrs. Boyer became aggressive. "And what does THAT mean?"

Keith took a deep breath before he spoke. "Personally -- and I think this is the Chief's position, too -- we're not much interested in crime in which there is no victim. She, for instance, is much more concerned about rape than porn."

"That's right!" Tracey asserted.

"But there's a connection!" exclaimed Mrs. Boyer.

"You THINK there is," growled Keith.

Tracey spoke up proudly. "Our Chief, you know, has almost wiped out rape in our city."

"Really?" said Mrs. Boyer dubiously.

"Oh, yes. Chief Kelly is famous in police circles for stamping out rape here. Surely you know that. In one year. Since she took office." Tracey was excited about it.

Mrs. Boyer's response was less enthusiastic. "Really?"

"Yep. We battled rape with publicity. Who, when, where, what, with what. Clinical details. All over the papers."

"The newspapers are full of that porn," Mrs. Boyer stated scornfully.

Tracey went on blithely. "All the details, assailants' names and next of kin, foiled attempts requiring gonad surgery, lenient judges, names of jurors -- plastered all over --"

Keith interrupted Tracey. "Yes. And we're not sure porn has much to do with rape."

"Oh, but it does, young man," Mrs. Boyer said grandly. "It does. All this filthy material flooding the minds of our young people -- it CAUSES rape!"

"Do you have children, Mrs. Boyer?"

"No. Reverend Boyer and I were not blessed in that way." She placed her hand on her chest in a pious pose. "And besides, I could hardly stand --" She stalled.

Keith grinned broadly at Tracey, who winked back at him. Mrs. Boyer shook herself and fluffed her hair behind her hat and then continued. "But I understand children. I've taught Sunday School for twenty-five years."

Keith and Tracey eyed each other again. "So what about the committee?" Keith asked Mrs. Boyer.

"I was going to invite you to serve on it with us. We've been a man short -- or a PERSON short, as we must say nowadays --" She smiled with saccharin sweetness at Tracey, who smiled back just as artificially. "Ever since poor Mrs. Flandermeyer passed away so suddenly." Mrs. Boyer displayed an instant of fake grief, with that hand pressed to her chest. "I'd like to see some new younger faces on the committee, persons who understand the modern young people and care about them and want them saved from all this filth that's drowning us all." She stopped and looked Keith frankly in the face. "Would you be willing to serve on the Mayor's Citizens' Censorship Committee?"

"Ahh --" Keith began. He looked to Tracey for help, but found none. "I'm pretty busy," he muttered. After hesitating he said, "I hate to say flat 'No,' but --" He faltered again. "Let me think about it. Since Titus died, we're a man short here, too. A person short, that is."

"Yes," burst out Mrs. Boyer. "Wasn't that a shame! He's the one I really wanted --" She caught herself and put her hand to her mouth. Tracey grinned at Keith, but said nothing. Mrs. Boyer tried to change the mood by reaching for the book on Keith's desk. "What's this?"

Keith grabbed the book quickly. "It's evidence. A new case." Then he studied Mrs. Boyer from a new angle. "Why?"

"I was attracted by the sub-title." Keith stared at her, perplexed. "On the cover," she continued.

Keith looked at the cover, and read aloud, "THIS'LL KILL YA. THE LAST WORD ON CENSORSHIP."

Mrs. Boyer was very smug. "Censorship interests me -- and you too, evidently." She leaned back in the chair. "Read me some of it."

"Really?" asked Keith. He glanced over at Tracey. Her expression dared him.

"Yes," said Mrs. Boyer. "I AM chairperson of the committee."

"Yes," murmured Keith. "So you are. Very well." He opened the book at random, near the front and read. "THE MAGIC WORD PAGES." He held the book closer, for fine print. "CAUTION! IF YOU BELIEVE IN MAGIC WORDS, READING THESE PAGES MAY BE HAZARDOUS TO YOUR HEALTH." Keith looked up. "It's really crazy," he warned Mrs. Boyer.

"Let's hear it," said Tracey, sounding eager.

Keith turned the page and read. "THE MAGIC WORD PAGES. THE FUNCTION WORDS." More fine print. "CAUTION! IF YOU BELIEVE THAT CERTAIN BODILY FUNCTIONS ARE BAD AND THAT THE WORDS REFERRING TO THEM ARE

MAGIC, READING THESE PAGES MAY BE HAZARDOUS TO YOUR HEALTH."

"Well, I declare," breathed Mrs. Boyer.

"It's like a poem, again," Keith stated. He read:

> I FART
> YOU FART
> HE FARTS
> SHE FARTS
> WE FART
> YOU FART
> THEY FART.

Mrs. Boyer began to gasp for air.

> I FARTED
> YOU FARTED
> HE FARTED
> SHE FARTED
> WE FARTED
> YOU FARTED
> THEY FARTED

Keith looked up furtively at Tracey and they both grinned.

> I SHALL HAVE FARTED
> YOU WILL HAVE FARTED
> HE WILL --

Mrs. Boyer interrupted, panting. "Oh. Oh. That's enough of that. Please."

"Everybody does," stated Tracey.

"What?" asked Keith.

"Pass gas!" teased Tracey, smiling broadly.

Keith turned the page and read.

> I PISS
> YOU PISS
> HE PISSES
> SHE PISSES
> WE PISS
> YOU PISS
> THEY PISS."

Mrs. Boyer breathed out with a long hiss. "What filth!"

"You think so?" asked Keith. He read further.

> I PISSED
> YOU PISSED
> HE PISSED
> SHE PISSED
> WE PISSED
> YOU PISSED
> THEY PISSED

Keith looked up. "And so on," he said. "Conjugates the verb, 'to piss.'" Tracey was grinning widely, and laughed aloud.

Mrs. Boyer turned on Tracey indignantly. "You LIKE this filth?"

"Like it?" pondered Tracey. "Not exactly. But it tickles me for some reason."

"And what do YOU think of it?" Mrs. Boyer demanded of Keith.

"Me?" he said. "Nothing much. Everybody farts. Everybody pisses. Those who don't die very shortly, when you remember the biology of it."

"It's absolutely horrible," Mrs. Boyer stated. She raised her voice. "Shameless. Filthy." She even gagged slightly.

"Read some more," Tracey said to Keith.

He turned the page. "O.K." He read. "THE FUNCTION WORDS CONTINUED." He looked up at Mrs. Boyer. "Coulda guessed it. You ready for this?"

Mrs. Boyer was fanning her face with her hand. "I doubt it," she gasped.

"Me, too," muttered Keith. He read.

> I SHIT
> YOU SHIT
> HE SHITS
> SHE SHITS
> WE SHIT
> YOU SHIT
> THEY SHIT

"Yes," said Tracey.

"Yes?" asked Mrs. Boyer, slouching a little in her chair. "Yes, what?"

"Everybody does," Tracey asserted.

Keith read further.

> I SHAT
> YOU SHAT
> HE SHAT
> SHE SHAT
> WE SHAT
> YOU SHAT
> THEY SHAT

He looked up, grinning. "Past tense."

Mrs. Boyer stood, and wobbled a little. "I think I'd better --" She flounced her dress, fanned her face, and looked toward the door to Tracey's office.

Keith waved his hand downward toward Mrs. Boyer. "No, Madame Chairperson. Wait a minute. Hear a little more." He smiled at her. "Find out about censorship."

Tracey chanted, wagging her head, "'He shat, she shat.' Has a ring to it. Almost poetic."

Mrs. Boyer gagged. "I'm afraid I'll vomit." She sat, taking deep breaths.

Keith turned pages while looking at Mrs. Boyer. "Sounds like you believe in magic words."

"Maybe I do," she replied, defensively.

"Well, I don't," Keith stated, shaking his head. He glanced down at the book. "Oh-oh."

"What?" asked Tracey.

"I'm not sure the Chairperson can handle this."

"Go ahead," Tracey urged. "She's a big girl."

Keith read.

> THE ENGLISH LANGUAGE NEEDS A STRONG MONOSYLLABIC ACTIVE TRANSITIVE VERB TO REFER TO SEXUAL INTERCOURSE. IT HAS ONE, BUT IT IS A MAGIC WORD.

"Stop it," begged Mrs. Boyer, leaning back, closing her eyes. "Don't."

Keith looked up. "Lady, you gotta be kidding! A word is just a word." He looked down at the page and read. "SEE THE SEX PAGES."

Tracey gave a little yelp. "Oooooh, there ARE some!"

Mrs. Boyer turned quickly to Tracey. "Some what?"

"Sex pages!" exclaimed Tracey.

"Oh! This is horrible," cried Mrs. Boyer.

Keith turned the page and read silently. Then he looked up at Tracey. "Here's an explanation."

"Read it."

"IN THE COLUMNS BELOW, THE ACCEPTABLE, PERMISSIBLE WORDS ARE ON THE LEFT, AND THE UNACCEPTABLE, IMPERMISSIBLE WORDS, EVEN IN

DICTIONARIES, ARE ON THE RIGHT." He turned his head as he read back and forth between columns.

FLATULATE	FART
URINATE	PISS
DEFECATE	SHIT
COPULATE	F---"

Mrs. Boyer's scream drowned out the last word.

"Stop!" she shrieked. "That IS enough!"

"They're just words," said Keith mildly.

Mrs. Boyer was panting. "I KNOW what they are," she groaned.

Keith looked down at the book. "Here's more explanation:

> THE WORDS ON THE LEFT ARE LATIN WORDS AND THOSE ON THE RIGHT ARE ANGLO-SAXON. THE ANGLO-SAXON WORDS BECAME MAGIC IN ENGLISH AFTER THE NORMAN CONQUEST OF ENGLAND IN 1066. THE LATIN WORDS WERE FOR THE POLITE, PROPER, GENTEEL AND GENTLE CONQUERORS. THE ANGLO-SAXON WORDS WERE FOR THE CRUDE, VULGAR, GROSS, DIRTY CONQUEREES. BUT THE

ANGLO-SAXON WORDS HAVE NEVER DIED OUT. INSTEAD, THEY HAVE BECOME MAGIC. CAUTION! USING THEM OR HEARING THEM MAY BE HAZARDOUS TO YOUR HEALTH.

Keith and Tracey laughed together. "That's pretty good!" exclaimed Tracey.

"Amazing," agreed Keith. "Imagine! Nine hundred years. More."

Mrs. Boyer wobbled to her feet again. "That book is shameless and horrible!"

"Madam, it's obviously ridiculous," stated Keith. "And you evidently don't like having your antiquated belief in magic exposed."

"It's dreadful," whispered Mrs. Boyer. But she sat. Keith turned several pages and read. "THE MAGIC WORDS CONTINUED. THE BLASPHEMY WORDS." He read fine print. "CAUTION! IF YOU BELIEVE THAT WORDS REFERRING TO THE DEITY ARE MAGIC, READING THESE PAGES MAY BE HAZARDOUS TO YOUR HEALTH. SEE ALSO THE FINDING OUT PAGES."

"Oh-oh," said Tracey. "Deity."

Mrs. Boyer brightened up a little. "Well. That's my husband's department," she said.

"Right," agreed Keith. "This may be interesting." He read. "THE FOLLOWING ANATHEMAS ARE TO BE READ IN A

SERIOUS EARNEST THREATENING SHOUT, STANDING WITH A FIST CLENCHED." He stood. "I'll do it," he said to Tracey.

"O.K.," she said. Then she added, "Be careful."

"Careful?" he asked. He looked at her and found her smiling warmly. "Oh, yes. Hazardous to our health." He read, shouting with a fist clenched above his head. "GOD DAMN THE KREMLIN!" He paused and looked at Tracey. "O.K.?"

"Sure," she said. "Is there more?"

"There's a whole bunch of 'em."

"O.K. Do 'em."

Keith shouted, with a fist raised and clenched, "GOD DAMN THE PENTAGON!"

"Oh!" burst out Mrs. Boyer. "That's horrible. Unpatriotic."

"One for each side," observed Tracey.

Keith shouted again, with his fist in the air, "GOD DAMN THE SALOONS OF THIS TOWN!"

Tracey grinned. "Well, I know people who feel that way." Mrs. Boyer nodded her head and touched her chest with her hand.

Keith shouted another one. "GOD DAMN THE CHURCHES OF THIS TOWN!"

Mrs. Boyer jumped up. "Oh! That is absolutely terrible. Sinful. Just horrible."

"One for each side, again," noted Tracey. Mrs. Boyer sat.

Keith shouted. "GOD DAMN ALL TERMITES! GOD DAMN ALL VOLCANOES!"

"Well, that's stupid," growled Tracey.

"There's one left," said Keith. "You ready?"

"Ready?" asked Tracey.

"Ready?" echoed Mrs. Boyer.

Keith shouted, with fist clenched, glaring at Tracey, "GOD DAMN YOU!"

Tracey jerked back as if struck. "Oh!"

Keith turned and growled at Mrs. Boyer with quiet intensity, "GOD DAMN YOU!"

Mrs. Boyer crumpled, closed her eyes and moaned very quietly, "Oh. Oh."

"Did you feel something?" Keith asked Tracey.

"No-o. It's just the idea," Tracey said, hugging herself a little and rubbing her upper arms.

"This is just terrible," Mrs. Boyer groaned softly. She sagged lower in her chair.

"I'm just reading what's here," Keith explained to Tracey.

"Well, yes. I know," Tracey said, but she sounded hurt a little nevertheless. "Is there more?"

"Looks like another explanation." Keith saw Mrs. Boyer sagging further. "Are you all right?" he asked her.

She pulled herself up, and fanned her hand in front of her face. "I'll live through it," she gasped.

"Read the explanation," said Tracey through tight lips.

Keith read carefully:

> THE EXPERIMENTER SHOULD KEEP CAREFUL TRACK OF ANY PERCEPTIBLE CHANGES IN THE KREMLIN, THE PENTAGON, THE SALOONS, THE CHURCHES, THE TERMITES, THE VOLCANOES, AND ONE'S COMPANIONS OR ENEMIES -- THAT COULD BE ATTRIBUTED TO THE USE OF THESE ANATHEMAS.

"You didn't mean it, then?" Tracey asked.

"Mean what?" Keith looked up at her, perplexed. She seemed cross and hurt. "That Goddam-you business?" She nodded her head. "I didn't mean anything. I was reading this thing. What do you think of it?" He tossed the book on his desk.

"It all seemed silly, until you did it to me," Tracey admitted.

"I didn't mean YOU," Keith explained. "I was just reading it."

"I know. It's O.K.," said Tracey.

"The whole thing is silly," stated Keith. "These anathemas aren't going to have any effect on anything at all."

"I don't think so, either," agreed Tracey.

"Nothing happened," continued Keith. "Nothing's gonna happen. The words are not hazardous to anyone's health. I don't believe in that stuff."

"Me neither," agreed Tracey. She turned to Mrs. Boyer, who was straightening her blouse and arranging her hat and hair. "How about you?"

"It's terrible," barked Mrs. Boyer. She struck the pious pose again. "The way evil books like that use wicked words --"

"Magic words," interrupted Tracey.

"-- and make fun of precious institutions like God and the churches and our armed forces," continued Mrs. Boyer.

Keith stood up. "More like making fun of what some people think they believe, if you ask me."

"Keith!" exclaimed Tracey.

"What?" he asked.

"Find the Sex Pages."

"The WHAT?" squealed Mrs. Boyer.

"It said there were some Sex Pages," Tracey explained to Keith. "Find 'em, and let's see what they say."

"You'll like it," Mrs. Boyer said scornfully to Tracey, "whatever they say."

"Probably," admitting Tracey, grinning broadly.

Keith sat again and reached for the book. "You're not afraid of the danger?" he asked Tracey.

"What danger?"

"Chief thinks this stuff is dangerous," Keith reminded her. "And something DID kill Titus."

"Well, it wasn't sex," Tracey said flatly. "Find 'em."

"O.K.," said Keith, paging through the book. "VIOLENCE PAGES. FINDING OUT PAGES. GUILT PAGES. SEX PAGES. Here we are."

He turned pages back one at a time. "Let's get to the beginning of this batch. Here we are."

He read. "THE SEX PAGES." Fine print. "CAUTION! IF YOU BELIEVE THAT FINDING OUT ABOUT AND THINKING ABOUT SEX AND SEXUALITY ARE INJURIOUS, READING THESE PAGES MAY BE HAZARDOUS TO YOUR HEALTH."

"Well, I don't," asserted Tracey proudly. "So read on."

"But I do," interposed Mrs. Boyer. "So maybe you better not."

Keith looked directly into Mrs. Boyer's face. "I'm gonna read 'em. You wanta go outside?"

Mrs. Boyer stared at Keith briefly. Then she said, "No. I'll stay. But it's awful."

Keith read.

I STAND NAKED IN FRONT OF A FULL-LENGTH MIRROR AND TAKE

MY PENIS IN MY HAND. IT FEELS WARM AND MY HAND FEELS COOL. I SQUEEZE MY HAND, THEN RELAX IT. SQUEEZE, RELAX, SQUEEZE, RELAX. MY PENIS BEGINS TO GROW IN SIZE. I FEEL IT PULSATE, FROM INSIDE, AND ALSO IN MY HAND.

Mrs. Boyer gasped aloud at the first use of the word, "penis." Then she giggled. She continued gasping and fanning herself. Keith looked up at Tracey. "You sure you want me to read this?"

"Sure I'm sure," said Tracey. "Go ahead."

Keith read further. "I BEGIN SLIDING MY HAND BACK AND FORTH --" He stalled and looked up again at Tracey. "Hey, this is kinda --" Again he stalled. Mrs. Boyer tittered, then began panting deeply and sagging a little in her chair.

Tracey cocked her head at Keith. "Go on. Read it."

Keith pulled on his ear. "Really?" He looked down at the book and read silently. "Hmm--, hmm--, aah--."

Mrs. Boyer began to moan, "Oh, oh, oh." Keith looked up at Tracey and shook his head, "No." He looked down and read silently.

Mrs. Boyer slumped down further and then groaned, "What happened?"

"It's just a male masturbation scene," announced Tracey.

Mrs. Boyer screamed and rolled off her chair. She knelt with her elbows on the seat of the chair. "Oh! Oh!" she cried.

Keith read aloud.

> NOW I'M SURE MY MUSCLES WILL WEAKEN, MY HEADACHES WILL WORSEN, THE CARTILAGES IN MY SPINE WILL SOFTEN AND CRUMBLE, AND HAIR WILL BEGIN TO GROW ON THE PALMS OF MY HANDS.

Tracey burst into a loud laugh. "Ha-ha! Wow! That's nonsense." Mrs. Boyer pulled herself up by the back of her chair.

Keith relaxed and had to grin. "That last part sure is stupid," he admitted.

Tracey reached a hand toward him. "Let me see that book."

He did not offer to hand it over. "You sure?" He turned to Mrs. Boyer. "You all right?" Mrs. Boyer nodded her head, "yes," and tried to smile, but managed only an ugly grimace.

Tracey waved her extended hand at Keith. "Let me read."

"Chief says it's dangerous."

"Nonsense," insisted Tracey. "Let me see it. Keep your place in it." Keith handed the book to her. She kept the place carefully, turned one page and read.

> I AM LYING IN A BATHTUB COVERED WITH WARM WATER AND BUBBLEBATH SOAPSUDS. I CLOSE MY EYES AND REACH DOWN BELOW THE HAIR OF MY CROTCH AND OPEN THE FOLDS OF SKIN WITH MY FINGERS. I WASH GENTLY ALL THE LIPS AND LAYERS. I PUSH THE END OF MY FINGER GENTLY ...

Mrs. Boyer let out her loudest scream yet. "Aaaiii! No! Stop!" Tracey read on silently, not looking up.

Keith got up and moved toward Mrs. Boyer. "Hey, take it easy!" To Tracey he said, "Cut it out, Trace." Mrs. Boyer emitted a long squeal, high in pitch, trailing down. Keith stared at her. Tracey continued reading silently. Mrs. Boyer's eyes were closed. As she ran out of air, she sucked in loudly, gagging herself, and began to choke and cough.

Tracey ignored her and said to Keith, looking up at him, "Listen to this."

Mrs. Boyer coughed and gagged and spluttered, "No. No."

Tracey read. "NOW I KNOW THAT I'LL BE TORTURED FOREVER WITH A

PERMANENT INSATIABLE EMBARRASSING ITCH IN MY CROTCH --" She slapped the book on her knee. "Oh, that's so stupid."

"What is?" asked Keith.

"That itch business. That comes from NOT washing down there. She was taking a bath!"

"Yeah," breathed Keith softly. "Quite a bath." He asked Mrs. Boyer, "You all right?" She nodded, "Yes," but didn't look it. Keith reached for the book. "My turn again," he said to Tracey. Then he looked at Mrs. Boyer, who was getting back into her chair carefully. "But I wonder if we should go on."

"Why not?" asked Tracey.

"This damn book doesn't feel dangerous to me. A little gross in mixed company, maybe. But Madame Chairperson, here --"

"I'm all right," Mrs. Boyer croaked hoarsely.

"So I should go on?" asked Keith.

"Sure," said Tracey.

Keith turned the page and looked. "Oh-oh."

"What?" asked Mrs. Boyer, warily.

"Our author conjugates the most magic word of all."

Mrs. Boyer began to slump again. "Oh, no."

Keith turned the page and looked. "Now our author describes it. Hmmm. Hmmm." He read. "HE INSERTED HIS THROBBING PHALLUS --" Keith looked up and asked Tracey, "You know that word?"

"Yep," said Tracey. "It's not his finger."

"Maybe you better stop," wailed Mrs. Boyer.

"Should I?" Keith confronted Mrs. Boyer directly.

She straightened up a little, failed to suppress a giggle, and then mustered indignation. "Yes! I mean, No! Go on. I'll suffer it through to the end." She held her hand to her chest.

Keith turned a page. "Let's see." He read. "I LOVE TO WATCH OTHER COUPLES AS THEY ENGAGE IN SEXUAL INTERCOURSE."

"Well, we know what that is," Tracey observed flatly.

Keith read on silently. "Now it repeats that sentence in Anglo-Saxon." He turned the page and read. "I LOVE TO ENGAGE IN SEXUAL INTERCOURSE WHILE OTHER PEOPLE ARE WATCHING." Mrs. Boyer began slumping and gasping again. "More Anglo-Saxon." He turned the page and read. "MY SISTER --" He stopped and looked up. "Incest."

"Yes," noted Tracey. "I understand it's quite common." Mrs. Boyer sagged and gagged.

Keith turned the page and read, "MY MOTHER THREW OFF HER ROBE --" He stalled.

"Aha!" crowed Tracey. "Freud's magic word."

"Yeah," said Keith, grinning. "Mother- ". He glanced up at Mrs. Boyer and caught himself.

"Wait," said Mrs. Boyer in a strained voice. She tried to stand, but crumpled over Keith's desk. He and Tracey stared at her. She gathered her strength and sat back again. Keith looked down and read silently, while Tracey glared at Mrs. Boyer.

"Our author doesn't let up," Keith announced. "Shall I go on?" he asked Mrs. Boyer. She nodded her head, "yes." She opened her mouth, but no word came out. She nodded more emphatically, "yes." Keith read. "I RUBBED THE HUGE ST. BERNARD UNTIL HIS PENIS PROTRUDED MORE THAN A FOOT. THEN I PULLED HIM OVER TO MY WIDESPREAD LEGS, AND --"

Mrs. Boyer let out a little yelp and slid sideways off her chair to the floor and rolled over onto her back with arms flung wide and her legs spread.

"Oh, dammit," growled Tracey.

Keith jumped up, slammed the book on his desk, ran to Mrs. Boyer, stood over her and glared back at Tracey. "It was too much for her!"

"Evidently," said Tracey, disgusted.

"That book IS dangerous!" yelled Keith.

"Nonsense," stated Tracey.

"Look what it did to her!"

"Pure nonsense."

"What'll we do?" Keith knelt beside Mrs. Boyer, reached for her wrist, grasped it, pressed it in several places. "Oh, dammit all!" He bowed down and put his ear on Mrs. Boyer's chest. He raised his head, then lowered it again. He snuggled his ear in her bosom, and then held it there. Mrs. Boyer opened her eyes, raised her feet and them dropped them. Keith raised up quickly. "You all right?" he asked her. Tracey leaned over and watched the proceedings on the floor from her chair.

Mrs. Boyer replied in a small weak voice. "I think I'll be all right." Then she raised her head off the floor, and asked in a much stronger voice, "What were you doing, young man?"

"Doing?" repeated Keith. "I was checking to see if your heart was beating!"

"And what else did you do, while I was unconscious?"

"He raped ME here on top of his desk," stated Tracey scornfully.

"Trace!" barked Keith. "Help me get her out of here."

Tracey got up reluctantly and stepped over Mrs. Boyer. "O.K. We'll put her on that cot in my office."

"Can you get up?" Keith asked Mrs. Boyer.

She sat up carefully. "Yes." She rubbed her head, and straightened her hat. "What a terrible book."

"Yes," agreed Keith.

"Don't be silly," Tracey said. They lifted Mrs. Boyer by the armpits and stood her on her feet. "Can you walk?"

Mrs. Boyer rubbed her bottom with her hand. "I think so. If you help me."

The three of them struggled to Tracey's door. As they went out, Mr. Boyer came through the door from the Chief's inner office. Keith returned, as Tracey was telling Mrs. Boyer, "You'll be all right."

"Your wife had a fainting spell," Keith explained to Mr. Boyer.

"Oh. Another one."

"We're sorry," Keith offered.

"Well, it certainly wasn't your fault."

"She's on a cot in my secretary's office."

"Thanks," said Mr. Boyer. "I'll wait with her a little while there, then, if it's O.K."

"Sure. It's fine." Keith picked up the book, as Mr. Boyer went into Tracey's office.

Three

Tracey entered Keith's office and found him sitting at his desk, staring out the window at the grey weather. She sat opposite him and reached for the white-bound book which lay on his desk. "Let me try another section," she said.

Keith stirred from his reverie and asked, "Did Chief put YOU on this case, too?"

"Me?" she asked, a little startled. "Oh, I'm on every case." She paged in the book a moment. "Here's something different. How 'bout a change of pace?"

Keith leaned back in his chair, and clasped his hands behind his head. "I'm sure ready."

Tracey read. "THE CENTER OF REALITY PAGES." She moved the book to make out fine print.

> CAUTION! IF YOU BELIEVE THAT RELATIVITY, RELATIVISM, FLEXIBILITY AND UNCERTAINTY ARE BAD AND THAT FIXED UNCHANGEABLE ABSOLUTE CERTAINTY IS GOOD, READING THESE PAGES MAY BE HAZARDOUS TO YOUR HEALTH.

She looked up. "Shall I go on?"

Keith sat up straighter and shrugged his shoulders. "Let's hear it."

Tracey read. "MOMMY AND DADDY ARE MORE INTERESTED IN EACH OTHER THAN THEY ARE IN ME."

"Hmp. Sometimes," observed Keith. "What did you say's the name of this section?"

"The Center of Reality Pages," Tracey reminded him.

"Change of pace, all right."

Tracey turned a page and read:

> HUMAN INFANTS ARE BORN WITH THE ASSUMPTION THAT THEY THEMSELVES ARE THE CENTER OF REALITY, AND THAT THE COSMOS REVOLVES AROUND THEM. IT IS USUALLY PAINFUL TO THEM WHEN THEY DISCOVER THAT SUCH IS NOT THE CASE."

Kent Boyer appeared in the doorway behind Tracey. He did not enter, but stopped and listened to the reading. Keith stared out the window. Tracey read on:

> HUMAN GROUPS USUALLY OPERATE FROM ETHNOCENTRISM. MANY CALL THEMSELVES 'THE PEOPLE' AND ASSUME THAT ALL

> OTHERS ARE NON-HUMAN. WHEN PERSONS DISCOVER THAT THEIR GROUP IS NOT THE ONLY GROUP THERE IS, AND PERHAPS NOT THE BEST EITHER, IT IS USUALLY PAINFUL. MANY NEVER DO DISCOVER THAT, HOWEVER. THE DISCOVERY IS WIDELY REGARDED AS DANGEROUS.

Keith stood and walked to the window and stared out. "Not sure I like that. Isn't our country the best?"

Tracey looked at him. "Best?" She hesitated, pondering it. "I don't believe so. Not really." She thought some more. "It's like this says." She slapped the book in her lap. "It's infantile to think so. It's really all relative."

Keith shook his head. "I don't like the feel of it."

"Says here that it'll be painful," Tracey said. Keith was still looking out the window and missed her grin. She read on:

> FOR AGES HUMANS ASSUMED THAT THE SUN AND PLANETS AND STARS REVOLVED, IN SOME FASHION OR OTHER, AROUND THE EARTH. WHEN COPERNICUS AND OTHERS PROVED THAT THE GEOCENTRIC VIEW WAS FALSE,

MANY HUMANS WERE VIOLENTLY DISTRESSED.

She turned the page. "FOR AGES HUMANS BELIEVED THAT THEY WERE THE SPECIAL MASTERPIECE OF THE CREATOR, AND WERE IN FACT LIKE HIM, OR HER." She looked up at Keith. "I like that. The Creator may be female."

Keith stared out the window, away from her. "It's pure junk. Nothing but philosophy."

"And what's wrong with philosophy?"

"It's stupid. I took a course in it once. The prof was a lazy fake. It's all worthless."

"You had a bad teacher," Tracey said.

Keith shook his head, "No."

"Philosophy is ideas," Tracey insisted.

"Ha!" exclaimed Keith. "Ideas that couldn't possibly matter."

"You don't think it matters whether people think their country is the best or not? What else causes wars?"

"I mean things like whether the earth goes around the sun or not."

"You don't think it matters?" Tracey asked.

"No, I don't." Keith was very flat about it.

Tracey looked up at the ceiling and thought it over. Then she stated, "I disagree. It does matter. It's better that we have it right. If the earth IS going around the sun, we should KNOW it. The truth is better than having an incorrect idea in our heads."

"O.K. O.K. I don't see how THIS section can possible be dangerous. Bore somebody to death, maybe."

"I disagree again. Ideas can be dangerous. What's a revolution?"

"Never mind. Read some more."

Tracey turned the page and read.

> FOR DECADES SCIENTISTS TRIED TO DETERMINE THE EXACT NATURE OF REALITY, BY DEVISING REPEATABLE EXPERIMENTS AND TESTING THEORIES WITH MORE AND MORE PRECISE MEASURING DEVICES. WHEN DR. HEISENBERG --

She hesitated over the pronunciation, but then proceeded. "WHEN HEISENBERG PROPOUNDED HIS UNCERTAINTY PRINCIPLE, THE SCIENTIFIC COMMUNITY WAS ASTOUNDED. HUMANS GENERALLY HAVE NOT YET LET THE IMPLICATIONS TAKE FULL EFFECT IN THEIR PSYCHES."

Keith interrupted her. "You getting this?"

"Sure," replied Tracey brightly.

"You are? Well, go on, then."

She read. "HEISENBERG DEMONSTRATED THAT THE LOCATION

OF AN ELECTRON AND ITS MOMENTUM CANNOT BE KNOWN AT THE SAME TIME. UNCERTAINTY LIES AT THE CORE OF REALITY." She slapped the book on her knee. "Say, that's really --" She turned in her seat and spotted Kent at the door and stopped in mid-sentence.

"What is it?" Keith turned to see why she stopped and saw Kent. He stood suddenly. "YOU'RE here!" he exclaimed.

Kent came in, smiling broadly. "I'm sorry. I'm afraid I'm guilty of eavesdropping."

"How so?" Keith asked.

"I'm fascinated by what you're reading."

"This?" asked Tracey, holding up the book. "You like it?"

"I'm afraid it's the reason I was so impolite." Kent had to grin.

Keith tried to restore a business-like mood. "You wanted to talk to me?" he asked Kent.

"Yes," Kent replied. "I understand my wife asked you to serve on the Mayor's Citizen's Censorship Committee."

"She mentioned it," Keith said flatly.

"That's why I came back. To urge you to join me on the committee. I'm on it, too, you know. And I need some help. And some companionship."

"What do you mean?" Keith asked.

"So many of them are so fanatical, so unbending, so SURE. Say! Maybe that's why I like Old What's-His-Name's Uncertainty Principle!" Kent grinned, and the other two smiled back.

Tracey looked down at the book and read the name. "Heisenberg."

"Yes," said Kent. "Good old Heisenberg. I'd sure like to hear more. What book is that?"

Keith reached for it, and said cautiously to Kent, "It's part of a case --" He hesitated. "Actually it has to do with censorship."

"May I see it?" Kent asked.

"Well," Keith drawled, stalling, "we're not -- uh, not finished with it yet." He looked over at Tracey.

Tracey stood. "Maybe I'd better get to my own desk."

"Be a good idea, Trace," Keith agreed. Tracey left to her own office, closing the door.

Kent stood in front of Keith's desk a little awkwardly. "Are you very busy?" he asked tentatively.

"How do you mean?"

"I'd really like to hear more of what you were reading, if you have time and don't mind sharing it." They looked at each other. "You said it was about censorship. What is it?"

Keith looked at the cover of the book. "It's called, THIS'LL KILL YA." Kent laughed, delighted. "THE LAST WORD ON CENSORSHIP," Keith continued, reading the subtitle.

"I love it!" Kent exclaimed, laughing. He sat and pointed at the book. "What you were reading sounded more like philosophy. You called it that, in fact."

"Yeah," said Keith. "It's the least interesting part. So far. If you ask me." He opened the book.

"Read me more," Kent begged. "Please."

Keith turned several pages. "Let's see -- oh, here's where we were." He read.

> MOST HUMANS ARE UNAWARE OF THE INTRICATE COMPLEXITY OF INTELLIGENCE THAT SURROUNDS THEM AND IS NOT RELATED DIRECTLY TO THEM, AS FOR INSTANCE IN A BEE HIVE OR AN ANT HILL OR A ROTTING LOG.

"Yes," exclaimed Kent. "Full of intelligent life."

Keith looked at Kent curiously, and then read on:

> THERE IS AN EXTREMELY INTRICATE PATTERN OF INTELLIGENCE GOING ON INSIDE THE LIFE-SYSTEM OF ANY HUMAN. EXAMPLES ARE THE ACTIVITY OF BLOOD CORPUSCLES, MUSCLE CONTRACTIONS TO EXECUTE THE

> SIMPLEST MOVEMENT, AND TEMPERATURE REGULATION. IN MANY CASES, IF NOT ALL, THERE IS MORE INTELLIGENCE DISPLAYED AT THE SUBCONSCIOUS LEVEL THAN ON THE DELIBERATE CONSCIOUS LEVEL.

"It's true," Kent asserted. "We think we're so smart. And the part of us that's unconscious is smarter than WE are."

Keith turned the page and read more.

> MANY HUMANS REGARD THEMSELVES AS UNIQUE AND VERY SPECIAL. THEY ALSO REGARD THEIR PLANET AS UNIQUE. EARTH IS THE THIRD PLANET CIRCLING A FIFTH-RATE STAR, ABOUT HALFWAY OUT FROM THE CENTER OF A GALAXY WHICH CONTAINS TWO BILLION SUNS. THE UNIVERSE CONTAINS TWO HUNDRED BILLION SUCH GALAXIES, THAT WE KNOW OF. THE LIGHT THAT WE NOW SEE FROM THE NEAREST OF THOSE GALAXIES LEFT THERE TWO AND A HALF MILLION YEARS AGO,

THAT IS, BEFORE THERE WERE ANY HUMANS.

"He's trying to make us feel small," Kent mused. "Relative."

Keith turned the page and read. "EXPERIMENTS WITH THE MIND INDICATE THE POSSIBLE EXISTENCE OF MYRIADS OF OTHER SEPARATE REALITIES, AS COMPLEX AND REAL AS THIS ONE WHICH WE AGREE TO CALL THE REAL REALITY. SEE --" Keith hesitated. "I don't get this."

"What is it?" Kent asked.

Keith read. "SEE THE A.S.C. PAGES." He looked up. "Sometimes it refers from one section to another, calls the different sections 'pages.' But what's 'A.S.C.'?"

"I'm not sure," Kent admitted. "But do go on."

"Weird," Keith murmured. He turned the page and read. "EVERYTHING IS RELATIVE. ONE'S POSITION IN SPACE CAN BE KNOWN ONLY RELATIVE TO THE LOCATION OF OTHER OBJECTS IN SPACE. BY ITSELF, AN OBJECT ISN'T ANYWHERE."

Kent grinned. "Yes. Perfect."

"WHO WE ARE IS DETERMINED BY OTHERS. BY ONESELF, ALONE, A PERSON ISN'T ANYBODY."

Kent jiggled up and down in his chair. "Yes!" he exclaimed. "Incredible! True! Beautiful!"

Keith stared at Kent's exclamations and shook his head. He had to smile. Then he read on, becoming more and more emphatic as he went. "THERE IS NO LAST WORD ON ANYTHING. NO FINAL STATEMENTS ARE IN! THE SUBTITLE OF THIS BOOK IS ITSELF IN ERROR."

"And what was that, again?" Kent asked.

Keith looked at the cover and read, "THE LAST WORD ON CENSORSHIP."

"Yes!" Kent cried. "No last word on anything!"

Keith quoted his last reading, raising a fist in the air, "NO FINAL STATEMENTS ARE IN!"

Kent leaned back, grinning broadly. "You like it, too," he said. "Even if it IS philosophy."

Keith closed the book. "Tell me, do you believe in censorship?"

Kent lost much of his enthusiasm immediately. "Well, I'm on the Mayor's Committee."

"Oh," said Keith. "So you DO, then." He paused. "Reverend Boyer --"

Kent interrupted him. "Call me Kent."

"Really?" asked Keith. Then he grinned and leaned forward. "O.K., Kent. I need your advice." Then he paused and rubbed his chin. At last he plunged. "Do you believe a book can hurt you?"

"Hurt me?" Kent repeated. "As a weapon, maybe --"

"Do you believe a person could be hurt, or even killed, by reading a book?"

"I never heard of such a thing. Of course not. What --"

Keith interrupted him. "Of course! You couldn't believe in such a thing, or you wouldn't be on the Censorship Committee!"

"What do you mean?" Kent asked.

Keith explained with animation. "You could not BOTH believe that reading a book could hurt you AND serve on the committee! 'Cause the committee members have to read 'em all!" Keith laughed boisterously. "So the committee is protecting people from what the committee members don't believe in!" Keith laughed more, but Kent was very sober.

"Maybe it IS having a bad effect on me," Kent said quietly.

"Bad effect?" Keith asked.

"I don't know, exactly," Kent admitted. "But something's been the matter."

"Like what?" Keith asked with concern. "You feeling bad? You look fine. Are you sick?"

"I'm sick of some things."

"Like what?"

"My job, for one thing," Kent stated.

"Oh, really?"

Kent stuck a finger down inside his clerical collar and yanked on it. "This damn collar!"

"REALLY?" Keith asked, surprised. "So you don't believe --"

Kent interrupted him. "In this position a person gets stuck with a lot of stuff he doesn't really believe in."

"Oh. Like what?"

"Like the benediction at all the boring banquets." Keith broke into another grin, but sobered when he saw how seriously Kent was feeling it all. "Or the opening prayer at the football game," Kent continued. "You don't believe in a lot of it, then," Keith said. "THAT'S why you like the relativity section."

"I'm sick of absolute final dogmatic statements," Kent asserted. "Believe-it-or-you'll-be-sorry stuff."

"Your wife --" Keith began, but then stalled.

"Agnes is a true believer," Kent stated wearily. They both sat in silent thought a moment. Then Kent pointed at the book on Keith's desk. "Where'd that come from?"

"We don't know," said Keith.

Kent leaned back in his chair. "Read me more of it."

Keith picked up the book again. "Some of it is pretty strong stuff. The Sex Pages --"

Kent interrupted. "Test me. See if I can handle it."

"O.K.," Keith said, with a little warning note in his voice. He opened the book. "One way or another, anyway, I need to find out what it says." He looked down. "Well, how 'bout that?" He looked up at Kent. "These are 'The Finding Out Pages.'"

"Good," said Kent. "I need 'em."

Keith read fine print. "CAUTION! IF YOU BELIEVE THAT IGNORANCE IS BLISS AND 'TIS FOLLY TO BE WISE, READING THESE PAGES MAY BE HAZARDOUS TO YOUR HEALTH."

Kent closed his eyes. "This is marvelous," he sighed.

Keith read more fine print. "FURTHER CAUTION! IF YOU BELIEVE THAT WHAT YOU DON'T KNOW WON'T HURT YOU, READING THESE PAGES MAY BE HAZARDOUS TO YOUR HEALTH."

"So help me," Kent affirmed, "I'm ready to find out."

Keith read. "WE ARE BORN BETWEEN SHIT AND PISS. SEE THE MAGIC WORD PAGES." He looked up. Kent was staring directly at him. "We read some of them, Tracey and I. Conjugates the verbs. Kind of pounds it into you and pounds the magic out." Kent continued staring, wide-eyed. "Your wife was here when we read that part," Kent continued. "She had a hard time --"

"I know that sentence," Kent stated.

"What sentence?"

"The one you read. About where we're born. Augustine, or somebody, wrote it. In Latin." Kent became more excited. "And it's true, too. We ARE born between shit and piss. It's literally --"

"Sir!" cried Keith, a little shocked.

"What?"

"Well, your language. I'd think a preacher --"

"You think a preacher doesn't shit or piss?" Kent cried. "Or that he got born some other way, down some tube that didn't lie between shit and piss?" He was waxing hot.

Keith was mollified. "Well, not really, but --"

"Then, read on," Kent said.

Keith looked down at the book, then back up at Kent a little dubiously. Then he read. "MOTHER IS A LIAR." He paused and then read another line. "FATHER DOES NOT KNOW EVERYTHING." He paused again and looked up. "It's printed like a poem."

"Read it," said Kent.

Keith read.

> THE DOCTOR IS A TORTURER.
> THE POLICEMAN IS A MURDERER.
> THE SOLDIER IS A MASS-MURDERER.
> THE BANKER IS A THIEF.
> THE PREACHER IS A RAKE."

"Ha!" exclaimed Kent.

"You like this stuff?" Keith asked.

"I wanta hear it."

"I don't like it," said Keith. "It's overdone. YOU'RE not a rake. Some of it is true, some of the time, but --"

Kent interrupted, gesturing for more, "Read on."

Keith read.

> THE HERO IS A P.R. PROJECT.
> THE ADS ARE FALSE.
> THE MEDICINE IS A HABIT-FORMING DRUG.
> THE FOOD CONTAINS POISON.
> THE VOTERS ARE SELFISH AND AFRAID.
> THE PRESIDENT IS A CROOK.

Keith slapped the book on his knee. "See!" he cried. "It's overdone. Just because we had one who was, he says everyone always is."

"He says the worst," Kent mused.

"I don't like it," Keith said.

"He says what we've been afraid to think about."

"It's subversive, if you ask me. Sometimes it's crazy, sometimes it's dull, sometimes it's -- well, dangerous," Keith insisted.

"Good books often are," Kent said. "Didn't it warn you?"

"Warn?" Keith asked. "Oh -- 'Caution' -- what was this one?" He flipped back a few pages and found the fine print, and reread it. "CAUTION!

IF YOU BELIEVE THAT IGNORANCE IS BLISS AND 'TIS FOLLY TO BE WISE --"

Kent interrupted. "Yes. If you believe that what you don't know won't hurt you -- we all do lots of that." He sat up straighter and mimicked someone, "'Don't disturb me with the facts.'" He imitated someone else, "'I don't wanta think about it.'" And someone else, "'Don't tell me. I don't wanta KNOW! I don't wanta find out.'" He sat back. "THAT'S the attitude that's dangerous. Not some book --" He waved at the book in Keith's hands. "Not some book that helps you find out, that says what you've been spending energy trying NOT to think about."

"O.K. O.K. I get your point," Keith said, grinning. "Take it easy." Kent grinned back. "Want more?" Keith asked.

"I sure do."

Keith turned the page and read. "THERE ARE NO ELVES." He looked up. "Another poem. Sometimes it's printed like a poem." Kent gestured for more, leaning back getting ready to enjoy. Keith read.

> THERE ARE NO ELVES.
> THERE ARE NO GOBLINS.
> THERE ARE NO FAIRIES.
> THERE ARE NO GNOMES.
> THERE ARE NO DWARVES.
> THERE ARE NO SPOOKS.
> THERE ARE NO GHOSTS.

> THERE ARE NO WITCHES.
> THERE ARE NO WIZARDS.
> THERE ARE NO DEMONS.
> THERE ARE NO DEVILS.
> THERE ARE NO ANGELS.

He paused, and then read more slowly. "AND THERE IS NO GOD." Keith looked up, eyes wide. "That's terrible."

"Is it?" Kent asked.

"Certainly, it is."

"Read on," said Kent.

Keith turned the page and read:

> HUMANS DESPERATELY WANT THE PROTECTIVE FATHER THEY HAD, OR PERHAPS DIDN'T HAVE BUT NEEDED AND WANTED, IN CHILDHOOD. THEY PROJECT THAT INFANTILE NEED AND WISH UPON THE COSMOS, AND CALL IT GOD THE FATHER ALMIGHTY. IT IS AN ILLUSION.

Kent was very calm. "Freud said that. Some while ago."

Keith was agitated. "You seem very cool about it."

"Is there more?" asked Kent.

Keith glared at Kent, but then turned the page and read.

"THE NOBODY-FOR-PRESIDENT CAMPAIGN SOME YEARS AGO CONTAINED GREAT INSIGHT. NOBODY WILL END THE WAR. NOBODY WILL BALANCE THE BUDGET. NOBODY KNOWS WHAT TO DO ABOUT INFLATION. THE INTELLIGENT VOTER WILL VOTE FOR NOBODY."

Keith looked up. "It's that subversive stuff again, encouraging people not to bother voting." Kent did not respond. Keith read on. "WILLIAM BLAKE USED THE TERM 'NOBODADDY,' LONG BEFORE FREUD WAS BORN, TO INDICATE THAT THE PROJECTED FATHER FIGURE WAS NOT REALLY THERE. NOBODADDY --"

Kent interrupted. "Nobodaddy. That's marvelous. Nobodaddy."

Keith read.

NOBODADDY KNOWS ALL YOUR TROUBLES. NOBODADDY IS IN CHARGE OF THINGS. THE WILL OF NOBODADDY SHALL BE DONE. THE WHOLE WORLD IS IN NOBODADDY'S HANDS. NOBODADDY IS CREATOR AND LORD OF THE COSMOS.

Kent leaned back and let out a long sigh. "Ahhhhh!"

Keith closed the book and stood up. "That's really bad business. It's making fun of God."

"Do you believe in God?" Kent asked.

Keith didn't answer immediately. "Well, I don't know," he said finally. "Sure, I do. I guess. Doesn't everybody?"

"No."

"I mean decent people. Uh -- well, I haven't studied it much, or even thought about it much really, but I don't think that stuff --" Keith pointed at the book on his desk. "That stuff shouldn't be printed."

"You think the Mayor's Citizens' Censorship Committee should advise the mayor to impound all copies and forbid the print and sale of it?"

"Well, I --" Keith stalled.

"Even if it's true!" Kent added.

"True! Don't YOU believe in God?" Keith was shocked.

"I don't believe in Nobodaddy. And I'm very grateful for the name. It clears a body's head, and maybe makes thinking possible."

Keith was stunned. "You're a preacher, and you don't believe in God!"

"I'm losing my grip on all those absolute final unchangeable certainties," Kent admitted. "And you know what? It feels good!"

"This IS a dangerous book," Keith exclaimed. "It can destroy people's belief in God!"

"Oh? Like yours?"

"No, YOURS!" Keith cried.

"Oh, mine was already in trouble. Praying at football games was especially damaging. What about yours?"

"My what?" Keith asked.

"Your belief in God. But I forgot -- you don't like philosophy. Maybe that means you don't like thinking."

Keith was stymied. "I -- I don't know." He had to grin. "I'll have to think about that."

Kent returned the grin. "What did you mean when you said, 'dangerous'?" he asked.

"There are allegations that this book can kill people. By their reading it," Keith explained. "The title says it, but I took it as a joke. 'THIS'LL KILL YA.'"

"It can't be meant literally," Kent stated.

"I'm not quite sure." Keith continued musing, aloud. "The sex pages can't really hurt anyone, although that's what any committee would go after. The violence was bad, maybe put bad ideas in people's heads. I don't like the philosophy --"

Kent interrupted. "But can it be dangerous, harmful, LETHAL -- to know? To read something and find out? I don't get what you're driving at."

"Neither do I," Keith admitted. "But I need help." At that moment the door to Tracey's office burst open and Mrs. Boyer barged in. She was still badly disheveled. Tracey stood in the doorway. "What's the matter?" Keith asked.

"I tried to tell her you were in conference," Tracey explained.

Mrs. Boyer barked loudly at Kent, "What are you doing in here?"

"Talking to Mr. Bright," Kent said calmly.

"Well, stop it," Mrs. Boyer ordered. "He's a bad person."

"Bad?" yelped Tracey. "He is not!"

Mrs. Boyer wheeled on Tracey. "You shut up! You're wicked, too!" Tracey's eyes widened and her mouth fell open in astonishment. Mrs. Boyer turned to Kent. "Come on, before they corrupt you any further," she ordered.

Keith became angry, and spoke sharply to Mrs. Boyer. "Why are YOU in here? What is it you want?"

"I came for HIM," she shouted, pointing a thumb at her husband. "And I came to tell you to forget the mayor's committee. You'd be a hindrance."

"Hindrance?" Kent echoed, in wonder.

"Yes," declared Mrs. Boyer. "He's not sure of the connection between rape and filth. He makes fun of the armed forces and God. He reads dirty books!" Tracey let out a loud laugh. Mrs. Boyer continued, a little more quietly, "We don't want him." She glared at Kent. "So, come on."

"Come on, what?" asked Keith.

Mrs. Boyer raised her voice again. "I'm talking to HIM!" she yelled at Keith, while pointing at Kent. She turned to Kent. "Come. We're leaving."

Kent spoke very calmly to her. "You go on, Agnes. I'm not quite finished."

"Not finished?" Mrs. Boyer was enraged. "What business do you have with HIM? Do you know what he did to me?"

"No," Kent said. "What?"

"He tried to --" Mrs. Boyer stalled momentarily. "Tried to -- He, he molested me!"

"How could he molest you when he was busy raping me?" Tracey demanded.

"Trace, stop it!" Keith ordered, annoyed. "I was checking to see if you were still alive!" he said to Mrs. Boyer.

"He had his cheek and his ear here --" Mrs. Boyer explained to Kent. "Here in my --" She stopped, holding her hand on her chest.

"He wasn't attacking you, I'm sure," Kent said wearily to Mrs. Boyer. "Now wait outside. Mr. Bright and I have business."

"What business could you possibly have with that -- that molester of righteous citizens?" Mrs. Boyer demanded.

Keith interposed. "That comes under the classification of his business," he told Mrs. Boyer. "And mine. Now wait outside, please." To Tracey he added, "Show her out, Trace."

Mrs. Boyer glared all around, red in the face. "Well," she puffed. "Well, I never --!" She couldn't finish.

"Never, ever, yet, Agnes, learned to tend to your OWN business," Kent concluded, sounding very weary.

That made her furious. She shrieked and spluttered. "What! How dare you speak to me that way!" She panted in rage. "I'll not allow --" She had to gasp for air. Tracey took her elbow and steered her toward the door. Mrs. Boyer got one last lick in for Keith. "Forget it! Forget the committee!"

"I'll try to," Keith muttered.

As Tracey propelled her through the door, Mrs. Boyer screamed at Kent, "You'll hear about this when we get home!"

"I suppose so," Kent said, very calmly. Keith closed the door. The two men looked at each other warily.

"Sorry," Keith finally said.

"Sorry about what?" Kent asked.

"That you have to put up with --" Keith hesitated. "On account of me, you get that kind of --"

"It's constant," Kent said, sounding very tired. "I'm disgustingly close to used to it." Then he brightened, pointing at the book on the desk. "But let's get back to that." Keith picked it up. "You said it was dangerous."

"Yes. Allegedly," said Keith.

"And you thought maybe I could help."

"Maybe." Keith sounded dubious.

"Ask me," offered Kent.

"You're on the censorship committee. You don't believe that YOU could be hurt by reading a bad book, or you wouldn't risk your life serving on the committee."

"Are you afraid of that book?" Kent asked. "The one I like so much?"

"Afraid?" Keith repeated, wondering to himself. "Not exactly. I didn't think I was at all at first. But strange things are going on." He slapped the book gently in the palm of his hand. "Chief thinks this is dangerous. One of our men was ready to blame several deaths on it. You sure you want to do this? You don't have to, you know."

"Do what?"

"Take this book and read it. Report back to me as a censorship expert as soon as you can. No later than tomorrow."

Kent became excited. "You're going to let me take that book with me? And read it? I'd be delighted."

"Be careful," warned Keith.

"Careful? What do you mean?"

"Don't get hurt," Keith said.

"You think that book could hurt me? You don't know how much GOOD it has done me already," Kent assured him. Keith handed the book over. "Thank you. I'm honored. Really. Delighted." He hid the book under his jacket. "I'll bring it right back. Tomorrow."

"Good. Remember, it's evidence. Government property."

"I'll take good care of it," Kent promised.

"And good luck!" Keith added.

"Thanks." They shook hands. Kent started through the door and then stepped back into the room. "I'll protect it with my life!" he exclaimed. Both men laughed as Kent went out and closed the door behind him.

Four

Keith sat at his desk, reading a newspaper. Chief Kelly barged in from her inner office. Keith stood up. "Good afternoon, Chief," he said.

"Yes," she replied, very business-like. "Sit down." They both sat. She looked him over very carefully.

"What's up?" he asked.

"I came to ask you," she said brusquely. "How d'ya feel?"

"Feel?" asked Keith. "I feel fine."

"You're O.K.," the chief said.

"Sure, I'm O.K. Why?" Keith was slightly puzzled.

"You read the book, and you're O.K.," the chief repeated.

"Oh. Uh --" Keith hesitated. "Not really. Not all of it." Chief Kelly looked intently at him. "Not yet," he added.

"Did it make you feel funny? Any bad effect, of any kind, that you could pinpoint?"

"Uh -- no. No, not really. Although Mrs. Boyer --" He stalled.

"Mrs. Boyer, what?" asked the chief sharply.

"She fainted while Trace and I were reading it." Chief Kelly snorted loudly. "The Sex Pages were a little too much," Keith added, with a little snicker.

"I'm not at all surprised," stated the chief. After a pause she asked him, "So why aren't you reading it now?"

"The book?" He hesitated. "Um, it isn't here."

"Where the damn hell is it?" barked Chief Kelly.

"I'm not exactly sure --"

"Not sure?" she interrupted. "You lost that book?" she yelled. "The evidence!" She glared at him. "You idiot!" She shook her head. "How could you lose such a thing?"

"I didn't really lose it," Keith explained. "I expected it back yesterday, or first thing this morning. But he hasn't come in. I'll have Trace call him."

The chief's voice became more shrill. "You let some one else have it?"

"Yes," said Keith. "I trusted him. He wanted to help. He seemed downright eager."

"Who has it?" barked the chief.

"Reverend Boyer," answered Keith.

"Kent! Kent has it!" Chief Kelly paced back and forth, glaring at Keith, berating him, pointing at him from time to time, very angry. "You let Kent take that book out of here! You shirk your own job, let someone else run the risks, endanger him, and who knows who-all? -- I can't believe such carelessness! Such negligence!"

"It wasn't negligence!" Keith protested. "He really wanted to read it. He's a censorship expert. I was enlisting the help of an expert. And he was so eager. I would have had to fight him offa that damn book. He LIKED it!"

The chief calmed down a little. "He did?" Then she toughened again. "But YOU didn't."

"Not much," admitted Keith.

"It frightened you," the chief accused.

"Not frightened, exactly," countered Keith. "It -- bothered me."

"So you let HIM take all the risk."

"I'm not sure there's any risk to it," said Keith. "This whole case is really stupid."

"You think so," said Chief Kelly.

At that moment Kent came in from Tracey's office, carrying a briefcase. Instead of his clerical garb, he wore levis and a chambray shirt. Keith reached across his desk and shook Kent's hand. "Hello, Partner! Good to see you. We were just talking about you."

"Glad to see you, too," Kent replied. "Beautiful day!" He strode to Chief Kelly and took her hand warmly. "Good to see you, Maureen. Sorry I'm late. I was held up. And I need to confer with my colleague, here," he added, nodding back at Keith.

The chief smiled warmly. "So I hear." She looked relieved. "YOU look well."

He held her hand a little longer than a normal greeting. "I am. I'm fine. Really fine." He certainly looked brighter and more cheerful than the day before.

"No ill effect?" the chief persisted.

"Of what?" asked Kent, laying his briefcase on Keith's desk.

Keith explained. "I expected you here yesterday. Chief and I were a little worried, because you had the book --"

Kent interrupted. "Oh, I had some unexpected chores to tend to." He opened the briefcase and pulled out the book. "And I didn't come right away because I wanted to read this." He handed the book to Keith. "I mean re-read it." He smiled broadly and rubbed his hands. "It's excellent," he stated.

"You think it is?" the chief asked.

"Yes. An absolutely excellent book," Kent repeated.

Tracey burst in yelling. "Chief! Keith! Look at this, in the newspaper." She stopped and stared at Kent. "Oh, my god, what happened?" She handed Keith the paper and put her hands to her cheeks.

Keith read from the paper. "Mrs. Agnes Boyer died unexpectedly in her home yesterday. The prominent civic leader will be buried in Utah, her home state. She was the wife of the Reverend Kent Boyer, of Providence Church..."

Chief Kelly sat abruptly, and stared at Kent. Keith dropped the paper and stood toe to toe with Kent. "Sir, your wife --" he began.

"She seemed all right when she left here yesterday," Tracey interrupted.

"Unexpected chores," Chief Kelly murmured, staring at Kent.

Keith questioned Kent directly. "Your wife is dead?"

"Yes," replied Kent. He went on, almost airily. "I found her dead yesterday morning."

"Tell us," Keith ordered.

"Tell you what?" asked Kent.

"The circumstances of your wife's death," the chief said.

"Oh," said Kent. "Not much to tell." He pulled a chair over. "May I?" he asked, and sat. He did not speak.

"Sir," prompted Keith impatiently. "Your wife."

"I found her in her room yesterday morning, at her desk, dressed. I could tell she hadn't been to bed at all."

"You and your wife didn't --" Keith began, and then hesitated. "Didn't sleep together?" he blurted.

"Are you kidding?" Kent asked. Then he resumed. "She was stiff already. Sitting straight up. Eyes staring straight ahead. Teeth clenched. Muscle here in her jaw --" He rubbed his own jawbone. "-- bulging out. Really odd. The undertaker told me she had bitten off a piece of her tongue." He paused.

"Anything else?" Keith prodded.

"Not really. Just frozen there -- with that angry, jealous, frightened look on her face. Oh, I saw it often enough, but this was the worst." He was musing, not grieving. "She was really stiff."

"What was she doing, at her desk?" asked the chief.

"Reading," Kent replied.

Chief Kelly glared at Keith, then turned back to Kent. "WHAT was she reading?"

"Porn," he answered. "What SHE called porn," he added a little scornfully.

"You don't call it porn?" Keith demanded.

"The definition of porn is always an opinion, isn't it? Even if it's a judge giving a legal opinion. Agnes and I didn't agree on porn, or on a lot of things."

"Kent --" said the chief tentatively.

"Yes, Maureen?" he answered brightly.

"Are you evading our questions?"

"What questions? Ask me," he offered very openly.

"Was your wife reading that book --" Chief Kelly pointed to the book on Keith's desk. "--that book which Mr. Bright so ill-advisedly allowed you to take out of here?"

"I'm not sure," answered Kent.

"You ARE evading," said the chief.

"Did you show her that book?" Keith questioned.

"She had a way of prying into everything. Found it on MY desk. Recognized it. Said she saw it here and had heard parts of it." Kent mimicked his dead wife. "'Simply dreadful.' 'Absolutely scandalous.' She was infuriated that I liked it. Said it showed how depraved I had become. But yet SHE wanted to read it."

Chief Kelly persisted with the interrogation. "When you found her dead --"

Keith interrupted and finished the question. "Where was this book?"

Kent hesitated just a second. "On the floor beside her chair."

The chief settled back, shaking her head. "I was afraid of that. That very thing," she added to Keith.

Keith questioned Kent. "Why didn't you report this to us at once?"

"Report what?"

"Your wife's death!" barked Keith.

"I called a doctor. He certified her dead. Heart failure, he called it. I called an undertaker. He took the body away -- to try to straighten it. What would I call YOU for?"

Keith stared at the book in his hand. "She was reading this --" He stalled briefly. "She died." He looked at Chief Kelly. "Do you think this is number five?"

"I don't know," the chief replied. "You shouldn't have let him take it out of here."

The phone rang. Tracey picked it up. "Police Department." She paused. The Chief shook her head at Keith. Tracey put her hand over the phone. "Chief, the mayor wants to talk to you, as soon as you're free. What shall I tell him?"

Chief Kelly stood and went to her door. "I'll take it in here." She stopped in her doorway and spoke to Kent. "I'll talk to you before you go." Then she glared at Keith. "And you, too." She went out. Tracey hung up the phone and went out, leaving the two men alone.

Kent stared at the closed door leading to Chief Kelly's office. "She's really upset," he said.

"Yeah," agreed Keith. "I shouldn't have let you take this damn thing outa here."

"Why?"

"It's dangerous," Keith stated.

"Don't be silly," said Kent. "It's wonderful."

Keith stood up. "I'm beginning to think it's part of a plot." He walked to the window. "It's subversive. It undermines people's faith." He paced restlessly from the window to his desk and back. Kent watched him without moving. "It puts bad ideas into people's heads. Stupid philosophy crap! And it kills people."

"Really?" said Kent, sounding slightly amused.

"I don't know how it does it," Keith continued, "but it kills people."

"Are you sure?" asked Kent.

"Mrs. Flandersomething on the bus. Then the bus driver. Then his wife. Then Titus. And now YOUR wife."

"No book killed Agnes," Kent stated flatly.

"We have to get to the bottom of this," Keith wailed.

"I agree," asserted Kent.

Keith ignored Kent's interjections. "Who wrote it? Who's in on this? Who published it? How?"

"How?"

"Who set the type? How did the type get set without killing the typesetter?"

Kent grinned broadly. "Oh, you think --"

Keith interrupted and continued with his wild questions. "Who proofread it? A lot of people have to read a book just to get it into print. If this kills everyone that reads it, how did it get printed?"

"Good question. And if --"

Keith interrupted again. "How many copies of this thing ARE there? Where are they?"

"Who knows?" mused Kent.

Keith opened the book and looked carefully at the print. "It may NOT be printed. May be one of those fancy new computer typewriters that look like print." He examined it carefully. "Looks perfect."

"It IS perfect," stated Kent. After a pause he continued. "So you think it could have been one person, being very careful --"

Keith interrupted once again. "Or it could have been done abroad." He brightened, pointing at Kent. "I bet that's it! Typesetters and proofreaders who don't know English! So they don't get hurt. Damned Communists! It's a Communist plot!"

Kent grinned widely. "You don't know how crazy you sound -- and how much like most of the Mayor's Committee."

"This isn't funny!" Keith barked.

Kent sobered. "No. I know." He sat up straighter. "Listen. I have another question."

"Yeah? What is it?"

"Can an author write a book without reading it?"

"Can an author --" Keith echoed. Then he wilted, and wailed, "I don't know. But I have to --" He paged in the back of the book. "Oh, my god! You unstapled the last pages!"

"I guess Agnes did."

"She read the last pages, and this is the book that, if ya read it -- all of it -- it'll kill ya." Keith lay the book on his desk.

"Don't be silly," said Kent, picking up the book. "Sit down." Keith sat, and looked around the room a little dazed. "You need to hear more of this."

"But it's dangerous!" yelped Keith.

"Then call in your secretary. She's a brave canary."

"Canary?" repeated Keith, puzzled.

"See if it hurts HER to hear this stuff."

"Oh." Keith thought a moment. "I'll ask her." He pushed the intercom button.

"Yes, Keith," Tracey's voice came in over the intercom.

Keith spoke into the intercom. "Wanta hear some more of that sex philosophy killer book?"

"I'll be right in." She sounded eager.

"You don't think it'll hurt us?" Keith asked Kent.

"Her, for sure not," Kent said.

"Oh? And me?" Keith yelped.

"I think you'll survive." Tracey entered and pulled out a chair and sat. Kent opened the book and flipped pages. "Ready?" he asked the other two.

"Yep," said Tracey. "You O.K., Keith? You look upset."

"Chief and I think this goddam book killed Mrs. Boyer," he replied.

"That's silly," Tracey said.

"So we wanted you in here while I read some more," Kent explained to her. "If you feel sick or injured at any time, let us know right away."

Tracey looked from one to the other. "You guys are crazy."

"It does feel foolish, now," Keith admitted. "It's almost embarrassing, Trace. If you wanta go back --"

"Oh, no," she said quickly. "Not for the world. I wanta hear it."

Five

"These are the A. S. C. Pages," Kent announced.

"You found out what that meant?" Keith asked.

"Yes. Altered States of Consciousness."

"Oh-oh," said Keith. "Dope."

"More like courage, maybe," Kent countered.

The men stared at each other a moment and then Keith said quietly, "All right. Read 'em."

Kent read. "THE A. S. C. PAGES." The next was fine print.

> CAUTION! IF YOU BELIEVE YOUR NORMAL STATE OF MIND IS GOOD, AND ALL OTHERS ARE BAD, READING THESE PAGES MAY BE HAZARDOUS TO YOUR HEALTH.

Then he held the book at a normal distance and read.

> I AM RUNNING, FLEEING A HUGE TIDAL WAVE THAT FOLLOWS ME. I AM TERRIFIED. THE ROAR IS DEAFENING. THE WAVE IS LIKE A

> MOUNTAIN. MY CHEST ACHES FROM GASPING. MY LEGS ARE BENDING WITH THE EFFORT. MY HIP JOINTS ARE SEPARATING.

"It's a dream," said Tracey.

"A nightmare," Keith corrected.

Kent read. "I TURN AND FACE THE WAVE, WAITING FOR IT TO ENGULF ME."

"I'd wake up," Keith interjected.

Kent read.

> THE WAVE GOES INTO SLOW MOTION, BREAKS IN FRONT OF ME, LIFTS ME SLOWLY IN WARM SOOTHING GENTLE ROCKING MOTIONS. IT CARESSES ME. I PADDLE AROUND IN THE WATER OF THE WAVE, CARESSING IT BACK.

"Oooh," cooed Tracey. "I like that."

"You would," said Keith. "Almost sexy, wasn't it?"

"Really!"

Kent turned the page and read. "I DREAMT I WAS A BUTTERFLY." He looked up at Tracey. "Maybe you know this one."

"Let's hear it," she said.

> I DREAMT I WAS A BUTTERFLY, AND NOW I CAN'T TELL IF I'M A MAN WHO REMEMBERS HE DREAMT HE WAS A BUTTERFLY, OR A BUTTERFLY NOW DREAMING THAT HE'S A MAN.

Tracey clapped her hands once. "Yes! It's marvelous!"

"It is?" asked Keith, looking at her.

"Sure, it is. How do we know that things really ARE the way we usually think they are?" Tracey was excited.

"Well, aren't they?" asked Keith.

"Who says they are? Or need to be?" Tracey mused. She looked at Kent. "I really like this stuff."

"Me, too," he agreed. He turned the page.

"Things better be the way they are," Keith asserted.

Tracey turned to him and smiled. "Do you hear how stupid you sound?" She mimicked him. "'Things better be the way they are.'" She continued, quite excited. "Of COURSE they're the way they are. But are they the way we THINK they are?"

Kent was turning several pages. "There's a lot of this altered state stuff. I liked it a lot. Maybe it'd bore you," he said to Keith. "You're not into philosophy."

Keith stared at Kent. "How can you be so calm?"

"Calm?" Kent asked. "About what?"

"Your wife just died," Keith said. "Under mysterious circumstances! And you sit there, and read that -- that WEIRD SHIT! And smile. And enjoy yourself."

Kent was very calm. "I don't think my wife died under mysterious circumstances. Her meanness was bound to catch up to her sometime."

"Read us some more," Tracey asked Kent. Then she turned to Keith. "Maybe the philosophy explains why he's so calm."

"Indeed, it does," Kent stated. He shook the book a little. "This has helped me figure out some things." Then he read. "MOST OF MYSELF IS UNKNOWN TO MY CONSCIOUS SELF." He skipped some and then read again. "ALTERED STATES HELP ME MAKE THE UNCONSCIOUS CONSCIOUS. EVERYTHING -- ALL VIRTUES, ALL CRIMES, ALL GOOD DEEDS, ALL BAD WISHES -- EVERYTHING A HUMAN BEING IS CAPABLE OF -- IS WITHIN ME." He paused, and skipped some text. "MY CONSCIOUS EGO IS A COMICAL CHARACTER -- SO SERIOUS, SO PROUD, SO SELF-IMPORTANT, SO SMALL." He paused again before continuing. "I AM LEARNING TO LAUGH AT MYSELF. AND

TO SEARCH AND EXPLORE --" Kent swept his arm grandly, and read in a quoting tone, "-- WHERE NO MAN HAS GONE BEFORE." He looked up and grinned. Then he read, "I AM NOT SO SURE ANY MORE. SEE THE CENTER OF REALITY PAGES." He was grinning broader than ever when he looked up. "Remember? Old Heisenberg?"

"He's where you came in," Tracey said, smiling at him.

"Right," said Kent, closing the book. "Excellent book." He lay it on the desk. "Thanks for letting me read it."

Keith roused himself. "Well, I'm in plenty of trouble with the Chief for letting you read it. Now you have to help me solve this case." He stood and proceeded in an interrogating tone. "Your wife read this book."

"Yes," said Kent. "Probably. Part of it, anyway."

"And she died."

"I found her dead yesterday morning," Kent repeated.

"Titus was found dead after reading it," Keith continued.

"I don't know about that," said Kent.

"You don't know either that that's what killed him," Tracey said to Keith.

Keith dropped his interrogator's air. "I know," he admitted and walked to the window.

"Maybe this will help," Kent volunteered.

"What?" asked Keith without turning.

"I read it," Kent asserted.

"Yes!" exclaimed Tracey eagerly.

"I read ALL of it," continued Kent. "Several times."

Keith turned. "And it didn't hurt you?"

"I didn't die," said Kent.

Keith resumed the interrogation. "But it DID hurt you."

"I'm -- different," Kent admitted, hesitantly.

"Different," repeated Keith.

"But I LIKE the difference -- in me," Kent continued. "And in the world. In everything!"

"What do you mean?" Tracey asked.

"Feels like freedom," said Kent. "Fresh air."

"Reading that book did something to you," Keith repeated.

"Yes," stated Kent. Then he pointed at Keith. "YOU should read it."

Keith recoiled. "But it's dangerous!"

"So is living," Kent said quietly.

"More philosophy!" Keith snorted scornfully.

"Really, you should read it," Kent repeated. "It would not kill you."

"Certainly not," said Tracey.

"It didn't kill me," Kent said. "It didn't hurt me physically in any way."

"See!" Tracey sneered at Keith.

"It only did me good," continued Kent. "It changed me. For some people, though, that's dangerous. Maybe --" He stalled briefly and then said softly what had just dawned on him. "For some people, maybe that's -- fatal."

"Fatal!" echoed Keith. He whirled on Tracey. "See!"

Kent continued musing aloud. "Some people can't stand to be changed."

"So the book IS dangerous!" Keith asserted again.

Kent picked up the book, partly distracted from the other two. He opened it to the last page and looked up at them. "I tell you, it did me good. It changed me. For the better." He ran his finger down the page as he proceeded. "The Magic Word Pages were like a colossal joke." He paused and moved his finger. "The Sex Pages I frankly liked. Agnes was never much interested in the real thing. Not at all lately. If I didn't get to read about it --"

Keith interrupted him. "O.K. O.K. The Sex Pages aren't dangerous."

Kent moved his finger down the page a little. "The Violence Pages were strong medicine."

"I thought so, too," Tracey interjected.

"But it's better to have it out in the open, better that it be conscious. You don't put that stuff in people's heads. It's already in all our heads. People who won't admit that, to themselves if not to anyone else, THEY'RE the dangerous ones."

Keith rubbed the back of his neck. "Never thought of it quite that way," he admitted.

Kent moved his finger again. "The Guilt Pages were like vomiting at last after trying hard for too long not to. The relief was a wonderful cure. I can't imagine who doesn't need it." He moved his finger again. "The Finding Out Pages excited me when you read them here. They still do. And yet they are simply stating openly thoughts that I've been afraid of for some time, and spending energy trying not to think. Now it's out in the open." He moved his finger once more and then lay the book down. "The Center of Reality Pages and the Altered States of Consciousness Pages open a person up, if he'll allow it. I couldn't stop it, and -- well, the whole thing changed my life."

"How did it?" asked Tracey.

"I've resigned from the church."

"You're quitting!" Keith exclaimed

"Yes," said Kent calmly. "Even if it IS unpatriotic to be a quitter. I have to --"

He was interrupted when the chief's door burst open. Chief Kelly barged in, obviously still worried. "Chief," said Keith. "He says he's quitting the church."

"Oh?" asked the chief. "That, too?" She pulled a chair up and sat. "The Mayor's puzzled about what's happening to his Censorship Committee. The ones that haven't dropped dead have resigned." She sounded weary.

"Right," affirmed Kent, almost proudly.

"You quit the committee, too?"

"Yep." Kent was smiling broadly. "That was one of my unexpected chores this morning."

"What's so funny," the chief asked Kent.

"Maureen, my sense of relief is so great, I can't help myself."

"And your wife not cold in the ground," accused Keith.

"She was cold long ago," Kent retorted and smiled warmly at Chief Kelly.

At last she spoke to him. "So you read the book?"

"Yes," said Kent. "ALL of it. And I'm not dead."

"But he thinks a book can change a person," Keith added, with an accusing tone in his voice.

"Oh, I know it can," Kent said confidently. "Sure, there are other things. But the book can trigger things, or be the last straw."

"And the last straw, for some people," Keith accused, "could mean --"

"Ha!" exclaimed Kent. "Maybe!" He was excited. "Maybe a book is like voodoo."

"Voodoo!" cried Tracey.

"Do you believe in voodoo?" Kent asked Keith.

"Of course not."

Kent turned to Chief Kelly. "Do you?"

The chief did not answer, but instead stood and walked to the window and looked out. Tracey spoke. "I don't know if I do or not."

"Do you?" Keith asked Kent.

"Uh -- I'm not sure," Kent replied. "Not really. Not for me, anyway. But I understand that for those people who DO believe in it -- it works."

"What do you mean, 'it works'?" Keith demanded.

"In Haiti and parts of Africa, voodoo works -- it can hurt people, KILL people -- or protect people. Because they believe it can." Chief Kelly turned from the window, very much interested.

"So what does that have to do with this book?" asked Tracey.

"Well, I was thinking," said Kent. "Maybe a page full of printed words will do what you believe they'll do."

"What does THAT mean," growled Keith.

"Believers in censorship -- TRUE believers -- are believers in sorcery."

"You haven't been believing in censorship for a long time," Keith accused.

"Of course not," Kent admitted. He picked up the book again. "This book was put together by a SORCERER."

"And he's trying to get certain people --" began Tracey.

"But he warns them," Kent added. "Time after time." He mimicked the readings from the book. "'CAUTION! READING THESE PAGES MAY BE HAZARDOUS TO YOUR HEALTH.' And always prefaced by, 'IF YOU BELIEVE...'"

"So --" Tracey began again.

"So -- if you DO believe, one thing or another -- in magic words, or that sex is bad, or that violent thoughts are bad --"

Tracey interrupted Kent. "Yes. And I kind of do, about the violence, I mean -- so those pages --"

Kent proceeded. "Or that altered states of consciousness are bad, or that FINDING OUT is bad --"

"It can hurt you," concluded Tracey.

"So it IS dangerous!" insisted Keith.

Kent opened the book near the back. "There's a section here called, 'THE PURPOSE OF THIS BOOK PAGES.' May I read it?"

"Go ahead," Keith said grimly.

"It's the last section," explained Kent. "The stapled part that Agnes opened." Keith started and straightened up. Kent read. "THE PURPOSE OF THIS BOOK PAGES." He adapted to fine print. "CAUTION! IF YOU BELIEVE IN CENSORSHIP, DO NOT READ THESE PAGES. THEY WILL BE HAZARDOUS TO YOUR HEALTH."

"No maybes about it, this time," Keith observed.

Kent read. "THE PURPOSE OF THIS BOOK IS TO REMOVE NOSEY BELIEVERS IN CENSORSHIP FROM THE GENE POOL."

"It's a threat!" exclaimed Keith. "Pure and simple."

Kent read on. "A PERSON MUST BELIEVE IN CENSORSHIP TO BE INJURED. AND A PERSON MUST READ IT, FOR IT TO HAVE ITS EFFECT."

"It says it right out!" cried Keith. "It admits it's dangerous!"

"It's been doing that all along!" Tracey exclaimed at Keith.

"Just a little more," said Kent. He read. "PERSONS WHO DO NOT BELIEVE IN CENSORSHIP WILL NOT BE INJURED IN ANY WAY."

"See!" Tracey sneered at Keith.

Kent turned the page and read.

ANY THOUGHT, WHICH ANY HUMAN BEING THINKS, IS ALREADY IN THE PSYCHIC PUBLIC DOMAIN. EVERYONE IN THE WORLD ALREADY HAS A HEADFULL OF GROSSITIES AND POTENTIALLY DANGEROUS THINGS INSIDE HIM OR HER. THE LESS CONSCIOUS ALL THAT IS, THE MORE DANGEROUS.

"It's true!" Tracey exclaimed. Chief Kelly studied the reactions of Keith and Tracey to the reading.

Kent proceeded.

> EXPRESSING WHAT IS WITHIN, IN SPEECH OR WRITING, AND DISCOVERING WHAT IS IN EACH OTHER, BY LISTENING OR READING, CAN ONLY MAKE US LESS STUPID, LESS UNCONSCIOUS, LESS UNCONNECTED TO THE REST OF OURSELVES AND TO EACH OTHER.

"More philosophy," Keith growled, dismissing it with a wave of his hand.

Tracey turned on Keith, thoroughly annoyed. "Well, LISTEN to it. Become less unconscious."

"'Less unconscious,'" imitated Keith, mocking. "What a stupid way to put it. Why not say, 'more conscious'?"

"Go ahead and say it, Smarty," cried Tracey. "But TRY it sometime, instead of labelling something you have to ponder for half a second 'philosophy' and refusing to think about it!"

Kent closed the book thoughtfully, ignoring the exchange between Keith and Tracey. "So, it IS dangerous," he mused. "Painful. Something in us doesn't want to grow. Doesn't want to find out." He was deep in thought.

"This book killed your wife!" Keith asserted loudly.

Kent roused from his thoughts. "Meanness killed Agnes," he said calmly.

Keith became more agitated. "I should arrest the book." Tracey laughed loudly. "I should -- er, confiscate the book, and arrest the author!" He glared at Tracey, and then wheeled on Kent. "Did YOU write this?" he asked, accusing.

"Me?" exclaimed Kent. "I wish I had." He picked it up. "I'd be very proud of it." He returned to his inner musing. "Maybe, now that I've quit, I will write something --"

"Something dangerous?" interrupted Tracey, almost teasing.

"Any good book is dangerous," Kent mused.

"I'm not sure I believe that. What can a book do to you?" Tracey asked.

"You have to read it to find out. But it CAN hurt you. You lose a kind of virginity."

"Oh!" exclaimed Tracey, and she blushed brilliantly.

"You're never quite the same again," Kent continued. "If you're really paying attention. Some little bit of the old stupider you -- is gone. Dies. Your mind is changed, expanded. Sometimes a little, sometimes a lot." He continued quietly, still musing. "And some rigid, little, brittle minds snap."

Keith became agitated again. "And the police should protect those people," he asserted.

Kent chuckled. "The police should protect the believers in sorcery -- from the sorcerers." Tracey laughed out loud. "Lots o'luck," Kent said to Keith.

The detective turned to his boss. "Chief, I can't make it out. Sometimes I think it's all a fake. All -- philosophy. Then I'm sure I should find and arrest the author. I didn't think I took censorship and the mayor's stupid narrow-minded committee seriously. But I'm pretty sure I think this book should not circulate."

"You ARE going to try to protect the sorcery people," Kent observed.

"You don't think we should?" Chief Kelly asked Kent.

"I say, let 'em defend themselves. If they don't want to learn things, they shouldn't read. This has the warning label on it and splattered all through it. 'CAUTION! CAUTION! CAUTION!'"

"So, what do I do?" Keith asked the chief. "Track down the author?"

"Imagine being the author of this," Kent wondered, tapping the book in his hand.

"You don't think it does harm?" Chief Kelly asked him.

"No," Kent replied. "I've said already, it does good."

"What about all the dead people?" cried Keith shrilly.

"You can't blame that on the book," Kent explained. "If someone jumps out a window, you don't blame the sidewalk twenty stories below for killing them. They didn't adapt to reality. They killed themselves."

"But this book?" insisted Keith. "It killed your wife!"

"That's not what killed her." Kent was very patient. "Look. Here's a marvelous book, the kind that opens your head, makes you think, makes you grow. It has labeled itself as such. My wife dedicated all her life to NOT growing, not learning, not opening up her head to anything -- in fact to CLOSING her mind and other people's, to PREVENTING growth and change. She picks up the book, ignores the warnings as not applicable to her, like she did about a lot of things, prepares to attack the author and anyone else who likes it, like me -- and her anger, her envy, her hatred, her arrogance, her narrowness all gang up on her and -- and she's excused from further participation in this reality. You can't blame the book for that -- she wasn't participating anyway, for a long time!"

Tracey became more business-like with Keith. "What do we know about the other alleged victims?" she asked.

"I've been working on that all morning," Keith said. He glanced over at the chief and then spoke to Kent. "While YOU kept the book." He replied to Tracey. "Didn't find out much. Mrs. Flandermeyer was on the committee."

Kent spoke up. "Just like Agnes, she was. They hated each other, they were so much alike."

"And the bus driver?" Tracey asked Keith. "And his wife?"

"We don't know much," Keith admitted. "Strong church members."

"There's Titus," said the chief quietly.

"Yes. Titus," echoed Keith.

After a silence, Tracey spoke. "Keith, I hate to say this. I know you liked and respected him. But Titus Cramp was a very narrow-minded man."

"Yes, he was," Chief Kelly agreed.

"He often told me he thought the world was going to hell," Tracey added.

"He hated young people," continued the chief. "You were an exception," she said to Keith.

"He never married. Never had kids," said Tracey.

"He told me there were simple old-time answers to every problem," remembered the chief.

"I heard him say that, often," Keith admitted.

"Old Heisenberg alone must have been hard for him to take," mused Tracey.

"Or the guilt pages," suggested Kent. "If you never look at yourself, the mirror can be --" He stalled.

"Dangerous?" asked Keith.

Kent had to smile faintly. "Yes. Maybe."

Tracey drew the conclusion. "So, Titus committed suicide, by reading a book he couldn't handle, after being warned."

"Could be," said Kent. "I'd still like to meet the author."

The room was silent. At last Keith spoke. "When's the first you knew about it, Chief?"

"The book?" Chief Kelly asked.

"Yeah. How did Titus get hold of it? Do you know?" The Chief did not answer right away.

"What's the matter?" Tracey asked finally.

"Sometimes I think maybe I should turn myself in," the chief said at last.

"Turn yourself in?" Keith asked. "For what?"

"Maureen, did YOU write this book?" Kent exclaimed suddenly, beaming at her.

"Uh -- not exactly," she stammered. "But --"

"But, exactly WHAT?" demanded Keith.

"I found it, one day -- that is, a handwritten manuscript of it -- in all my notes." She looked at Kent. "For that course we took at the University." She turned to Keith. "It was a philosophy course."

"Where we met, Maureen," Kent said and smiled warmly.

"You two DO know each other, don't you," Keith said suspiciously to Kent and Maureen.

"Oh, we've admired each other for quite some time," Kent said openly. "Very chastely, you understand." Keith stared frankly into his face for a moment. Kent turned to the chief. "But tell us about the book!"

"I found it in my notes, like I said. I have no idea where it came from, how it got there.

Remember," she said to Kent, "one day I asked in class if anyone had lost any notes?"

"Yes, I do remember that. I didn't know what you were referring to. What happened?" Kent prodded.

"No one claimed them. I read the manuscript very carefully." She smiled faintly at the group. "I wasn't killed. I saw it as a joke. Decided to have it printed. Now I wonder if I wasn't trying to get rid of some of my frustrations over that damned censorship committee. And other things. But then, it got out of hand, out of my control --"

Keith interrupted her. "Chief, I gotta do this. Were you interested in him --" He jerked his thumb at Kent. "When you printed up that thing?"

"Well, it's hard to tell what to count. I met him at the University and liked him. We had a drink together once after class. I attended the church once, but couldn't stand --" She stalled.

"His wife," Keith concluded.

"Yes," Maureen said softly.

"Chief, that could be made into a motive." Keith hesitated. "Why did you do this?"

"I didn't really intend to DO anything. I saw it as a joke, mostly."

"Titus thought it was a serious case," said Keith.

Chief Kelly hesitated before continuing. "After the book got out, strange things started happening. I put Titus on the case. I had to find out. I couldn't just keep it all to myself. I felt, sometimes, like a -- like a, well --"

"A murderer!" whispered Keith. "You don't need to incriminate yourself any further at this time, Chief."

"Incriminate!" Kent burst out. "So she didn't like my wife. Lots of people didn't like her. Hundreds. Thousands. She butted in everywhere! I didn't like her any more myself."

Keith pointed an accusing finger at Kent. "So you plotted --"

The chief interrupted. "No. He did not. Not at all. He was a perfect gentleman at all times. And I didn't plot anything, either. It was that nosey Mrs. Flandermeyer --"

"Just like Agnes, she was," Kent repeated.

"Found it on my desk one day when she was in here berating me for letting college students fornicate. I see now I should have kept it from her. But I couldn't resist letting her take it. After all, she was a censorship expert!"

"That's what happened to ME!" Keith exclaimed. "With HIM!" he added, pointing at Kent. "I couldn't stop him."

After a long silence, the chief asked Keith, "So, am I under arrest?"

Keith thought some more. "I don't know," he murmured, staring into her face. "What for?"

"You tell me," she said.

Keith mused aloud. "Murder? No evidence. Not of any kind, really. No judge would -- no jury -- it would be a joke. Conspiracy? No evidence."

Tracey broke the spell, getting up. "I should say not. You're all being very silly. A book is a book. Murder and conspiracy and all that are something else." She turned to Kent and Maureen. "Didn't you two have a lunch date? You better get going."

Kent offered an elbow to Maureen. "Shall we?"

The chief took his arm and smiled. "Yes. Let's." She turned back to Keith. "We can wrap this up later."

Keith picked up the book from his desk. "Nothing to wrap, Chief. That I can think of." He looked her in the eye. "Why don't you take the afternoon off? Trace and I'll hold things down here."

"Good idea, I think," the chief agreed. "We'll see you later then." She and Kent went out through Tracey's office.

SIX

"Well," said Tracey. She looked at the book in Keith's hand. "There's the book that, if you read it, it'll kill ya. What d'ya think of that?"

Keith was very sober. He spoke quietly. "I don't know. Really. I thought it was silly, but it's not. Not by a long shot." He scratched his head. "It's very strange." He opened the book and turned a page at a time, several times. "This goddam book --" He looked up at Tracey's face. "Can you watch things here alone for a while?"

"I think so," Tracey said. "Where are you going?"

Keith nodded at Tracey's door. "I want you to go out there and lock me in here." He hesitated, studying the book. "I'm going to conduct an experiment."

"Oh," said Tracey very quietly. "Read that book."

"Yes," asserted Keith. "I'm going to read it, every word of it, cover to cover. I'm going to let it do -- whatever."

"Good," breathed Tracey. Then she spoke more firmly. "I'm proud of you. You're brave."

"You think maybe it'll kill me?" Keith asked, seriously.

Tracey smiled. "No --" She stalled briefly. "Not in the usual sense," she added.

"What the hell does THAT mean? You philosophers!"

"Remember what Kent said," Tracey told him seriously. "The old you, the old stupider virgin -- dies."

"He means I'll change," Keith said flatly. "Be changed."

"Yes," whispered Tracey.

"Well, get going, then, and close me in here." He sat up straight in his chair, with the book held in his two hands at his desk. Tracey patted his shoulder and went to the door. "I can hardly wait to see what it does to me!" Keith exclaimed.

Tracey smiled warmly at him and went out the door. Keith read in silence.

ACTS

OF

GOD

1

Mount St. Helens blew her top today, spewing lava in rivers down her rocky flanks, where life forms had not yet fully recovered from her last eruption. Thousands of tons of thin powder ash have been blown aloft, drifting northwestward.

At least one team of American geologists is feared lost. The team was studying the growth of the dome inside the crater. Latest radio messages from the team referred to "additional activity, probably in the next several weeks." There is no indication that any of the scientists had any thought of an eruption as sudden and violent as that in progress at this time.

Traffic in the western half of the State of Washington has been restricted to government officials, forestry personnel, law enforcement officers and workers in defense installations. An unofficial report from Seattle indicates heavy ashfall in the area, with as much as six inches reported in the vicinity of the Boeing Aircraft Facility.

1A

The National Guard has been called out in the State of Washington to assist state and local police in restoring order in the wake of yesterday's eruption of Mount St. Helens. Successive earthquake shocks and continuing outpourings of lava and airborne ash indicate that the volcano is still active.

The ash is interfering with the movement of emergency vehicles. Panic-stricken survivors have swamped medical facilities, and closed down telephone communications altogether. All lines are flashing the familiar busy signal. Poison gas emitted from the crater's mouth has hampered scientific study by helicopter. Two feet of ash is reported on the ground in Seattle.

The President has not yet declared Washington a federal disaster area. "To do so," he is quoted as saying, "would give the liberals one more budget-busting weapon. If everyone does his part, out there, there'll be no need of interference by any federal agencies." He is reported favorably disposed toward Boeing's preliminary request for cost-overrun expenses due to damages caused by thirty inches of volcanic ash in and on everything at the assembly plant outside Seattle.

2

Minor earthquakes have been reported in a wide area in the Rocky Mountain west. While no single quake registers very high on the Richter scale, the number of virtually simultaneous reports is regarded as unusual by a team of seismologists stationed near Yellowstone Park.

It is feared that Old Faithful, the famous geyser at Yellowstone, may have been affected by the quakes. The spout of steam and hot water, which has appeared regularly every ninety minutes for more than a hundred years, has not been seen since the first quake reports, twelve hours ago.

More alarming affects of the earthquakes are suggested by reports from isolated sections of eastern Wyoming. Independent scientists at Colorado State University in Fort Collins, report "explosions, not earthquake tremors," and "radioactive material in the atmosphere," over eastern Wyoming. It is feared that one or more Minuteman missiles may have been detonated in their silos, with subsequent leaks into the atmosphere. One visiting Japanese scientist speculates that none of the shocks felt in recent hours were earthquakes, but that all of them are from U.S. nuclear bombs exploding in their underground missile silos.

The Pentagon has not issued any official statement. One spokesman said, off the record, when asked about nuclear explosions, "It's communist propaganda and nonsense. They can't fire until we fire 'em." Travelers are advised by state police of Wyoming and Colorado to stay out of the area.

Federal geologists in Washington, D.C., have stated that the tremors are aftershocks from the recent eruptions of Mount St. Helens, one thousand miles away.

3

Communications have broken down between an area of West Virginia and the rest of the nation.

No television or radio station is currently broadcasting. Some telephone lines appear to be open, but no persons respond to any signal. Several airliners have flown into the area, on commercial schedule, but have not yet reported back. The Eyewitness TV helicopter reporter also flew to the area an hour or so ago, but has not yet radioed any type of report to this station.

The Governor has dispatched State Police teams to the area, but the office has received no report back from any of the teams as yet.

3A

Panic threatens a large area of Appalachia this evening, especially southeastern Ohio, most of West Virginia, southwestern Pennsylvania and western Virginia.

There is no sign of life in an area two hundred miles across. The center of the area is located at Institute, West Virginia. The president of Union Carbide Corporation, currently visiting in Bhopal, India, tending to legal matters, was contacted by radio-telephone by this reporter. He refused comment, beyond saying, "Not every unfortunate incident can be blamed on our company. We'll stand on our record."

Meanwhile the national guard forces of several states are trying to cordon off the affected area. The difficulty is that no one knows how large the area is, or how much larger it may become, or what is causing the cessation of life activities.

No one can be raised by radio, or telephone. Commercial flights have been canceled. Traffic toward the area is stalled in massive tie-ups.

The President does not regard this as a federal disaster, as yet. "We'll need to make additional studies," a spokesman told this network.

3B

The chemical leak from Union Carbide at Institute, West Virginia, poses a threat of widespread proportions. One part per million of isopropyl-ortho-benzocyanate causes instant death to all life forms, animal and vegetable. Scientists are concerned that wind currents may not disperse the danger, but simply spread it. Life in the oceans could be endangered, some scientists report. Tobacco farms in North Carolina are at risk, as well as what's left of oyster beds in the Chesapeake Bay.

The president has dispatched the 29th Infantry Division, equipped with the latest cost-overrun gas masks, into the area, to prevent looting, especially at military installations.

4

Hurricane Nancy has wrecked havoc in the Caribbean Sea. The greatest damage seems to have occurred in Cuba and in Honduras, at opposite edges of the huge cyclone, which registered winds up to 120 miles per hour.

The aircraft carrier KITTY HAWK capsized off the coast of Honduras and then ran aground on a jungle beach. All hands are reported lost, including some Americans. The newly-built military installations in Honduras are reported very severely damaged, also, with great loss of life suffered by the mercenary troops stationed there, including some Americans.

In Cuba, the American naval base at Guantanamo, an American facility since the days of

Teddy Roosevelt, received a terrific pounding, by wind and tidal wave. Rescue vessels, sent from Puerto Rico, report difficulty in locating the site, with all man-made installations, and much of the beach and coastal areas washed out to sea.

The president announced that this government will not tolerate such attacks on American facilities and personnel. "Castro and Ortega will pay for this," he said, from his vacation ranch in Texas.

Camp David has been temporarily closed because of the threat of poison gas from Institute, West Virginia.

5

The IRS reports absolutely no receipts in recent weeks from either of the states of Washington or West Virginia. "This situation is absolutely intolerable," a spokesman said. "The production of this year's quota of MX missiles is falling behind, because of this shortfall. Corrective steps must be taken immediately."

When the president was asked about disaster relief funds and efforts to relieve suffering in the affected areas, he replied, "Suffering is all right. But not paying taxes is a federal crime, which we will prosecute to the fullest extent of the law."

6

A cold front moved out of the Rocky Mountains into the Central Plains this afternoon, spawning several severe thundershowers and tornados.

Minor wind damage to rural communities was reported in Kansas and Oklahoma. In the Texas panhandle a freak tornado touched down twice in the same area, on the outskirts of Amarillo, doing extensive damage to the nuclear missile assembly plant there.

The L-shaped plant has been totally demolished. No buildings are left standing. An unspecified amount of fissionable material is reported "missing," as well as an undetermined number of plant workers, including some Americans.

Eyewitnesses, coming to work for the swing shift, report that the tornado struck the west end of the east-west wing of the plant, and, we quote, "just chewed hell out of it, all the way across to the outer fence. Then the funnel raised up off the ground and sailed around toward the north, screaming and whistling and wailing like a freight train out of control. Then it touched down at the north end of the north-south wing and wiped out the other half of the installation, leaving the site clean as a bone."

The funnel reportedly then rose and headed east, according to eyewitnesses. Radioactive material has been found on the ground as far away as central Oklahoma, according to state police there. Travelers are advised to avoid the entire area, until clean-up crews can gather the radioactive material, and assess the damage. One Oklahoma native called this reporter to say, "I used to think the Russians were a threat to us. Now I'm not sure. My grain elevator and my oil wells are a radioactive mess, and the Russians didn't do any of it."

A reporter asked the Roman Catholic archbishop of Amarillo if he believed that Tornado X, as it is being called locally, was a case of direct divine retribution. The archbishop replied, "I have been convinced for a long time that nuclear weapons are immoral and contrary to God's will for man and the world. But a tornado is a natural phenomenon." When asked about the strange path of the tornado, the archbishop said, "X marked the spot," and declined further comment.

7

Hurricane Nancy, which caused such heavy damage to Cuba and Honduras, is now punishing Louisiana. The storm seems to have stopped on its northward path, with the eye located about fifty miles south of the former site of New Orleans. Torrential rains and record high tides have moved the seacoast inland fifty to one hundred miles. The Mississippi River bed is now a maritime estuary all the way to Natchez.

Loss of life is feared high, including some Americans. High winds have hampered rescue operations by air. Low-lying areas have simply disappeared under the surf.

The Weather Bureau has been seeking the cooperation of the Pentagon in finding a way to move the eye of the storm, or perhaps break it up. The President has approved a plan to drop a one hundred megaton nuclear bomb into that area, in hopes of causing the storm to move on. Some members of Congress are reported to have objected privately, but no official moves to stop the planned bombing have developed. Congress will not resume formal sessions until a week from Monday, following the current vacation recess. The Senators from West Virginia and Washington State are reportedly still in the capital, but could not be reached for comment.

7A

The Pentagon reported today that a B-1 bomber flew over the eye of Hurricane Nancy and dropped a "nuclear device," but that no explosion occurred. Officials from General Electric, General Dynamics and E. F. Hutton refused to comment.

Meanwhile, the coastline continues to move further inland. Mobile and Baton Rouge are gone. Vicksburg is now experiencing tidal movement in what used to be the bed of the Mississippi River.

8

The State Highway Departments of both New York and Pennsylvania have closed all tunnels and bridges leading into and out of the state of New Jersey.

More than a dozen simultaneous outbreaks of deadly nerve gas poisoning have been detected in New Jersey, and authorities are not certain that the sources have been located. For many years New Jersey has been at the head of the list of states harboring the nation's most dangerous toxic chemical dump sites. Local environmentalists, critical of the pace of federal clean up, have told this network, "New Jersey is famous as a bedroom community for New York and Philadelphia. But it's really the cloaca of the entire nation. We get everything that everyone else finds poisonous. Now chickens have come home to roost."

Experts are disagreeing on the source of the nerve gas. "It goes through here on tank trucks and railroad cars, every hour of the day and night, every day of the year," one said.

"God only knows what chemical process goes on under those land fills," said another. "Covering that stuff up with dirt does not make it chemically inert."

"We've observed its effect on the health and intelligence of nearby residents, over the decades, and no one was disturbed. Why is there such a fuss now?" a third expert asked.

This particular outbreak of chemical poisoning seems to attack the human nervous system, leading to the nerve gas designation. But it may not be the same nerve gas purchased by the Pentagon for defense purposes. Scientists, including chemical specialists, have been called to the scene, but the closing of the tunnels and bridges may hinder a prompt response to that call. Meanwhile, the death toll has been reported in the hundreds in several cities: Princeton, Cream Ridge, Tea Neck, Hopatcong and Hackensack, including some Americans.

9

Hurricane George, spawned rather suddenly in the Gulf of Mexico, or perhaps sighted late by employees of the now privately-owned Weather Bureau, struck the Houston area with full force last night, causing great damage to the NASA facilities and great loss of life, including some Americans.

The administrator of NASA gave an interview from a large refugee shelter in a church in San Antonio, in which he stated that the damage was so severe that it may bring to a halt the next series of space experiments planned for NASA. "We were already in budget trouble," he told our reporter. "Now we may have to scrap the whole project." The agency was going to study the effect of the moon and its phases on the weather here on earth, especially in North America. Many citizens have been questioning for some time the value of these very expensive activities. No figures on the estimated cost of rebuilding the facilities are available at this time.

9B

Hurricane George, after devastating Houston, Texas, has veered eastward and back out to sea over the Gulf of Mexico. Meteorologists regard this as a very unusual path. The hurricane is regaining strength and moving slightly south by east.

9C

Hurricane George slammed into the Gulf Coast of Florida, on an east southeast track, and has plowed across that state all the way to the Atlantic Coast. The storm has spawned more than two dozen tornados, which have torn up unusual quantities of sand, in effect digging a channel across from west to east. Miami and Lake Okeechobee are now located on a newly-formed island, which appears to be sinking. Flooding, along with the violent tornado damage, has taken a great toll of lives, including some Americans.

The storm has destroyed the space facilities at Cape Canaveral. The commander of the base there stated, "Thank God, there wasn't a vehicle on the pad at the time. The tower has been destroyed, but it usually is, at every launch. We'll just have to build us a new one." The commander refused to comment on any rumored budget problems.

10

A freak tornado wandered east of the Appalachian Mountains yesterday and touched down near the nation's capital. A spokesperson for the now privately-owned Weather Bureau told this network that the appearance of a tornado that far east was very unusual and probably illegal. The funnel struck the headquarters of the U. S. Department of Defense, so-called, a huge office complex popularly called The Pentagon, after the shape of the original floor plan of the building. Not one stone has been left standing upon another. Normal life in the capital city has been hampered by the quantity of paper strewn in the streets and lawns and into the Potomac River. The death toll from the tornado has not yet been determined, but it is assumed that it included some Americans.

10A

In a nationally televised TV interview, the chairperson of the American Friends Service Committee was asked to comment on the recent destruction of the Pentagon. "We live in very difficult times," she stated. "We need to decide how we can best help each other solve the problems that life presents. And we need to quit presenting each other with additional problems." When asked if she thought the tornado was a case of divine retribution, the Quaker leader said, "We all need to learn how to help one another, rather than blame one another, or hurt one another. God is usually brought in as a way of trying to fix blame on someone. Times are such now that we need to forget all that and ask each other, 'How can I be of help?'"

11

Early reports from New Mexico indicate volcanic activity in a wide area north and west of Albuquerque. One unofficial comment from the office of the State Police said, "I'm afraid we've lost Los Alamos." The governor's office in Santa Fe stated that the new volcano may have been "awakened by that Federal Geothermal Project in the Jemez."

A group of federally funded scientists have been studying methods of harnessing geothermal energy in the Jemez Mountains. The mountains were originally formed by volcanic lava flow, and are full of hot springs. "The heat which makes that water hot comes from the underlying volcano. Those guys have disturbed a sleeping giant," added the governor's spokesperson.

11A

Forest fires are raging over an area one hundred miles square, northwest of Albuquerque, New Mexico. The Jemez Caldera, the collapsed cone and mouth of the ancient volcano that formed the Jemez Mountains tens of thousands of years ago, is once again a seething, overflowing lake of lava, fire and sulphur. Lava has filled all the canyons in and around Los Alamos, and fire has destroyed all mesa-top buildings and forest growth, with great loss of life, including some Americans. The top-secret Los Alamos Scientific Laboratory has been totally destroyed.

The lava flowing to the east has blocked the Rio Grande. The water strikes the hot lava and is turned entirely to steam, which is carried aloft and eastward by the prevailing westerly winds.

Torrential rains are reported in eastern New Mexico, Kansas, Oklahoma and Texas. Local flooding is already a serious problem in some areas of those states, as rivers have risen far above flood stage and remained there since the rains began.

12

The president announced no more natural disasters for this fiscal year. All the funds have already been disbursed, mostly for increased administrative salaries for the heads of the various federal relief agencies. "Don't expect much in the new budget for next year, either," he added.

12A

It has been a week since the arrival of the first troops, transferred from Germany to New Mexico to fight the forest fire still raging out of control over an area the size of Bavaria. Bad morale has been reported among the troops. "What do we know about forest fire fighting? It's an Indian's job."

Troops also report supply problems. "You can't live off this land. It's Scorched Earth now, and was a desert to start with. Besides, our paychecks are late."

12B

The contra troops, American-trained Somocistas from Nicaragua, have been flown to coastal areas of Alabama and Georgia, now that Florida is gone, to control looting and patrol the new coastline. Many of them note that they have returned to the same paramilitary camps in which they received their original formal training. Some of them have attempted subsistence farming, but with only moderate success. Most of them have formed nomadic groups of bandits, committing rape, theft, arson and murder across a wide area of what is left of southeastern U.S. "It's just like home," one bandit said. "Except here we don't get free supplies and equipment added."

13

Reports from eastern New Mexico describe new seismic activity in the area of Carlsbad. The caverns, one of the most popularly visited national parks in the country, have been closed. "The elevators are out of order, and at several places the path down has been cut off by shifting rock," a ranger reported.

Additional news from Carlsbad reports the release of some radioactivity into the atmosphere from WIPP, the nation's disposal site for all the radioactive waste from all weapons facilities and all nuclear powered electric generators. Local residents are reported fleeing in alarm, but officials have released reassuring reports, stating that "not very much" radiation has escaped. "We're staying on top of it, monitoring all changes," a spokesperson announced. "Besides, that stuff has a half-life of only fifty thousand years, so the panic is definitely out of proportion to the danger. It's the sort of thing that often happens when nuclear power is involved."

The leukemia rate in the Carlsbad area had been reported at triple the national average, even before the earthquake, but officials dismissed that as co-incidence. "There is no scientific proof that this stuff is in any way dangerous," the same spokesperson added.

14

Geologists are rushing to the newly formed west coast of this country. The San Andreas Fault has given way, "from stem to stern," as one scientist put it. Half of California is gone, according to one unofficial report, with considerable loss of life, including some Americans.

Scientists are hampered in their studies by almost continuous aftershock activity. "This isn't just an earthquake. This is an immediate demonstration of the truth of the theory of plate tectonics. All the land west of the Fault is disappearing under the North American plate, east of the Fault. We can see the land moving."

Officials have tried to instruct surviving inhabitants of the disappearing area not to move eastward, toward the fault, but rather westward to the coast, and into the ocean on whatever will float, where they can be picked up by the Coast Guard, which has temporarily suspended its normal anti-smuggling activities. Terror has immobilized many. Others refuse to leave loved ones, or treasure of one kind or another.

The president is reported to be shaken, but determined to carry on. He has blamed this disaster on the international communist conspiracy. "The spies stole the secrets of our seismologists, and figured out a way to trigger this. But they'll not get away with it. I will not be the president who lost California. We shall be avenged."

The International Red Cross, the Red Crescent, the Red Hammer and Sickle and the Red Star of David, as well as UNICEF and other world relief organizations, have all offered their resources for humanitarian aid, but it has been refused. "America doesn't need help," stated the president. "We're the ones who give help, when it is to our advantage to do so. We don't need anyone coming here and telling us what to do."

15

Three agribusinesses have filed for bankruptcy in the Iowa dust bowl. These are not your ordinary incompetent Farmer Jones and Farmer Brown and Farmer Green. These are Birdseye, Safeway and The Great Atlantic and Pacific Tea Company. Drought records are being set in Iowa, according to the privately-owned Weather Bureau there. Food riots in major towns and food raids on granaries have become so common, local and network news no longer report them all.

16

After careful research by this network's investigative team, rumors of an escaped killer algae are now confirmed. Genetic Engineering, a top-secret government project in eastern Kentucky, has reported manpower difficulties, due to the chemical accident in West Virginia some months ago, and due also to some unaccountable interference in the company's experiments. Whatever the cause, independent scientists have now confirmed the presence of a new species of algae in the creeks and rivers downstream from the facility. This new algae crowds out all other plant growth in the streams and within ten feet of the water's edge. Also the new strain appears to be poisonous to all animal life, not only as food, but to the touch as well. Several children have been found dead in their swimming holes, not victims of drowning, but of an extremely fast-working poison.

Panic is spreading throughout the area. The Environmental Protection Agency has indicated an interest in studying the matter, if budgeting can be arranged for next fiscal year. Meanwhile, terror-stricken and infuriated mobs have attacked several federal facilities in the vicinity, reportedly aroused by the attempts of the president to make a joke of the matter. "I can handle killer algae. Or even killed parsnips and killer rutabagas. I'll become alarmed when we have to worry about killer lettuce."

17

With all the natural disasters on the domestic front, coupled with the sale of the Weather Bureau, American scientists had not observed the sudden melting of a large portion of the north polar ice cap. High tides were dismissed as freak local phenomena. But now it is incontrovertible -- coastal cities are in very serious trouble. Downtown areas are flooded twice a day, by high tides. Manhattan Island is underwater most of the time. Other cities affected include Boston, Atlantic City, Philadelphia, Wilmington, Baltimore, Washington, Norfolk, Charleston, Savannah, Galveston, and Portland, Oregon. Some scientists fear inland river and lakeside cities will also be damaged as the rate of flow of major rivers is altered.

The Sixth Fleet has been recalled from the Mediterranean and has been assigned to the Coast Guard, to help find and define and defend the coast. The Coast Guard has already reported a sharp decline in its own anti-smuggling activity. An official spokesperson stated, "There's hardly any smuggling going on. They're all a superstitious bunch, and they're saying to us and to each other, 'That damn country's bewitched!' They don't wanta come near the place."

18

With no budget with which to repair recently damaged military installations, and no will to resume foreign imperialist aggression abroad, and serious talk in Congress about abolishing the department, the Secretary of Defense resigned today. "There's nothing left worth defending," he is reported to have said.

Foreign aid measures have been laughed off the floor of Congress for many months. Israel has returned the West Bank to the Palestinians, since the required Pentagon support for holding it has not been forthcoming. U.S. military bases in the Philippines have been closed. The governments of South Africa, Guatemala and El Salvador have fallen into the hands of the people of those countries, since Pentagon opposition to such developments has been ineffective. With the cessation of the killing and destruction in those countries, a rising standard of living has been observed.

18A

In a surprise move, the president appointed the Chairperson of the American Friends Service Committee to the post of Secretary of Defense. He admitted that she was not his first choice, but that none of the businessmen to whom he offered the job would accept it.

The new secretary pledged that she would transfer all efforts and "whatever's left of the budget" into a program of general public assistance. "Some might want to call it a War on Disaster program, or a War on Suffering, but we Quakers dislike the military analogy. Suffice it to say, we will be doing all we can to help all of us help each other."

19

The president, who once stated that no place on the surface of the planet would be lost while he was at the helm, has just signed a bill, allowing nine states to secede. He denies that he is presiding over the dissolution of anything, but the map of the nation has been changed, and history with it.

The state of WASHINGTON is uninhabited, covered by one to three feet or more of volcanic ash. Scientific studies, when they are resumed, will be administered by Oregon and Idaho, jointly. An imaginary line now divides what used to be Washington between the other two states.

WEST VIRGINIA is likewise uninhabited. No scientific teams have expressed any interest in investigating. The president of Union Carbide has remained in India. On maps, the area of West Virginia has been returned to Virginia.

NEW JERSEY has been divided between New York and Pennsylvania. Most of it is under water. The old coast line is now claimed as territorial waters.

DELAWARE, RHODE ISLAND, FLORIDA and LOUISIANA are under water.

Two-thirds of CALIFORNIA has been gone for some time. The remainder will be added to Nevada and Arizona.

UTAH has been allowed to secede, by vote. The former governor has been proclaimed chief elder of the new theocratic state. His parting words to the mother country were, "We'll not be part of a nation that refuses to defend itself from foreign aggression wherever it occurs in the world. If Lesotho can do it, so can we!" There is talk of plans to build a wall around the new nation.

New Mexico has voted to declare itself a nuclear-free zone. Several members of Congress proposed expelling that state from the Union, for such defiance of federal policy, but the debate turned into a laughing interlude of comic relief, and in the end no vote was taken. "They are the LEAST nuclear-free zone on the planet. Who are they kidding?" "They started it. Did they think they could finish it?" "'Land of Enchantment,' they call themselves. They're enchanted all right, and nuts. Crazy."

20

This nationwide TV and radio network is about to be dismantled, going the way of many other national institutions, including the Weather Bureau, the Federal Housing Authority, the Federal Reserve Bank System, American Telephone and Telegraph and others. On this last broadcast, we will attempt to summarize recent developments and the outlook for the future. We only wonder who's out there able to hear us.

The nationwide grid of electrical power can no longer be maintained.

The use of the computer, and the telephone, is now limited to local activity, and only in non-devastated areas.

The highway and railroad systems can no longer be kept in safe usable condition.

Federal payments for welfare, housing, pensions of various sorts, military personnel and dependents, medical care, and food stamps are no longer forthcoming.

The reduced standard of living has caused great suffering in some sectors of the population.

Subsistence farming on small plots seems to be on the increase, but food riots and raids on storage facilities hamper production and distribution.

The feared invasion from abroad has not materialized, from any direction. Other nations have reportedly cut back on wasteful military expenditures, and revised their priority lists. Flooding of coastal cities world wide, and the need to adapt to the loss of American military expenditures abroad, have brought about widespread and far-reaching changes in the economies of most of the nations of the world.

Local governments in what used to be the United States are stronger, providing basic survival assistance to citizens. Many of those local governments have formally renounced war as an instrument of public policy. "We are all in this together," is a phrase often overhead. "Nobody's any better than anybody else." "We either all of us make it, or none of us make it." "We have a helluva lot of work to do."

Cleaning up the environment seems to be second on everybody's list of priorities, right after food provision. Small farmers report remarkably fresh fertility of the soil, in many areas, probably caused by all the volcanic activity. "There is work for everybody," a local farmer stated. "Grab a shovel. With enough shovels, and enough shovelers, we'll make it."

We close this broadcast with a paraphrase from a former president of this former country:

"The Almighty has his own purposes. Woe unto the world because of offenses, for it must needs be that offences come, but woe to that man by whom the offence cometh. If we shall suppose that the American military empire was one of those offences which, in the providence of God, must needs come, but which having continued through His appointed time, He has now willed to remove, and that He gives to all of us these terrible disasters as the woe due to those by whom the offence came, shall we discern there any departure from those divine attributes which the believers in a living God always ascribe to Him? Fondly do we hope, fervently do we pray, that this mighty scourge of disasters may speedily pass away. Yet if God wills that they continue until all the wealth piled by the imperial victims' hundred years of unrequited toil shall be sunk, and until every drop of blood drawn with the lash shall be paid by another drawn by some act of God, as was said three thousand years ago, so still it must be said, that the judgments of the Lord and true and righteous altogether.

"With malice toward none, with charity for all, with firmness in the right as God gives us to see the right, let us finish the work we are in, to bind up the nation's wounds, to care for him who shall have borne the battle, and for his widow and orphans, to do all which may achieve and cherish a just and lasting peace among ourselves and with all nations."

SOLILOQUY WITH FIVE INTERRUPTIONS

SOLILOQUY
WITH FIVE INTERRUPTIONS

I've had a lotta birthdays, but I think this is the first one I've ever celebrated all by myself. Gettin' back to basics, here in my little one-room adobe house. Everything I have is right here in sight, except the garden outside. And it's rainin' hard out there just now. Has been, since day before yesterday.

Usually someone's around for my birthday. Family or someone. But I guess not this year. So, I'll have to decorate my cake for myself. Cute little candles Rachel found somewhere. She's a sweetheart.

Family's all gone -- or gone away. Son Lamech died five years ago. Wife number seven died last year.

Now there was a woman. You ever heard of seventh heaven? Well, I know all about it. Wonderful woman.

Nice little candles. Grandson and all his family left about a week ago. Said they were going on a trip. I didn't pay much attention exactly where. We weren't thinkin' of my birthday. At least I wasn't. Little Japheth wanted 'em to take me along, I remember, but I didn't want to, and his daddy obviously didn't want me to either.

Well, let's see how they look lit. Here we are -- me, myself and I -- all together on my birthday.

Baked the cake last evening. Baked it myself. Without a wife, and family all gone, a fella learns to do things for himself. MY grandfather always said, "If you want a job done and done right, do it yourself." 'Course, it's nice to have someone do FOR you, too. But when it's not in the picture --

Ahh, that does look nice. Big fat cake and lotsa cute little candles all lit up and shining bright.

I've got a no-fail recipe for cake. Yep. This cake right here. Perfect every time. You know, PERFECT -- unless you wanta impress somebody. Ha-ha. My fifth wife always said that.

"Life's a real kick in the ass," she used to say -- she talked like that -- "if you let it get to be important. But if you're just sailing along enjoying, not trying for special effects, not trying to impress anybody -- then it's great." That's what she said, and she sure thought so -- Ahh, I remember her -- what a woman.

I was gonna make pancakes, one for each year, like the old story says, but how could one old man like me all alone eat that many pancakes. Hell, it'd take all day just to COOK 'em, no-fail, or no.

Pretty cake. Well, many happy returns of the day, and all that. "May you have many more." Ha! That's gettin' to be a laugh. How many more? How many's enough?

Well, c'mon, Oldtimer. Make a wish and get on with it. Let's see... Close your eyes... What do I wish?

I guess that doesn't change much over the years. Peace. And love. World sure needs it. And I need it. Take a deep breath and blow!

Seems too bad there's no one to share it with. Lemme check out the window.

Nice rain. Unusual, though, for around here. It's been raining for a week -- hard like that. It'll be good for the garden. Sure hope it's raining upstream, up in the mountains -- so we'll have water in the ditches all season. Bad business trying to garden here without water.

Life's funny, y'know. Like the rain -- it often comes too much at a time. I remember how my grandfather used to joke about it. Some newcomer'd ask him, "How much rain per year do you get around here, Jared?"

He'd say, "Oh, about seven inches."

"Really?" the newcomer'd say, "that makes this officially a desert then, doesn't it?"

Grandfather'd ignore that and look off remembering and say, "Yeah, about seven inches a year -- I remember last year -- yep, I remember the afternoon it came!"

Too much at a time. Like apples. If the apple tree bears apples, you have tons of apples,and so do the neighbors, and so does everybody, and you can't GIVE apples away.

But this is unusual -- to rain this much, this steady.

Well, back to the cake. May as well serve myself -- What? Who's there?

JUDE [voice outside]: Just me'n Rachel, Oldtimer. [OLDTIMER is delighted and hops to the door.]

OLDTIMER: Hot dog! Guests for my birthday. [He lifts the wooden bar and opens the door.] Come in, Neighbors! Really glad to see ya! [JUDE and RACHEL enter. They have on sopping plastic raincoats, and their shoes are muddy.] Don't worry about the mess. It's raining! That always makes a mess around here. Naw, don't worry. It's clean dirt. C'mon in. Have some birthday cake.

RACHEL: Is this your birthday, Oldtimer? [She's worried, trying to be pleasant through the fretting.] What a day for it.

OLDTIMER: It's a great day for it! I'm really glad to see ya both.

JUDE: Happy Birthday, Oldtimer. [They shake hands.] How many is it?

OLDTIMER [turning to RACHEL, opening his arms. He wants a hug from her.]: Too many to tell. [He and RACHEL embrace warmly.] Thanks for coming. Really. [He pulls a bench over toward the cake.] Here. Have some cake with me. I was just cutting it.

RACHEL [Looking at JUDE]: Do we have time?

JUDE [Worried, too]: I don't know. I guess maybe.

OLDTIMER: C'mon -- take off those new-fangled raincoats and sit and have birthday cake with an old man. [He sits on his stool and begins to cut the cake. They obey him, but look very worried.] What's the matter with you two? Don't let a little rain depress you. [He hands RACHEL a piece of cake, then licks his fingers.]

JUDE: You haven't heard?

OLDTIMER: Heard what? [He cuts another piece of cake.]

JUDE: We have to evacuate.

OLDTIMER: Evacuate? Who says so? [He hands a piece of cake to JUDE.]

JUDE: The authorities. We have to leave today.

OLDTIMER: Leave? Where to?

RACHEL: The mountains.

OLDTIMER: Mountains! My God, that's MILES -- and why? What is all this?

JUDE: They say there's gonna be flooding. The river can't handle all this rain. [He stares out the window from his bench.] I never saw so much rain ...

OLDTIMER [Thoughtfully]: Yeah, I never did either. [More animatedly] But that's no reason for some county sheriff to get all huffy and order everybody out! Evacuate.

RACHEL: You better come with us, Oldtimer. We'll look after -- I mean -- well, I hate to think of you having to find your way to the mountains all alone.

OLDTIMER: Rachel, Honey, I know where the mountains are. They were there before you were born, and they haven't moved.

JUDE: Everybody's supposed to head for higher ground.

OLDTIMER [He goes to the window and looks out. Pause.]: They really expect flooding?

JUDE: Yeah. It's raining too much.

RACHEL [Trying to brighten the mood]: This is a very good cake, Oldtimer. Can I have the recipe?

OLDTIMER: Sure! You really like it? [He comes back to the cake and cuts another piece.] Lemme try a piece of my own cake. [He takes a big mouthful.]

RACHEL: Where's Japheth?

OLDTIMER [Chewing and swallowing first]: Family took him on a trip. About a week ago.

JUDE: Where to?

OLDTIMER: I don't know. They wouldn't say. [More thoughtfully] Now that you ask, it was a little -- well, maybe peculiar. Just said they were going on a trip. I wasn't very curious. I knew I wasn't going, y'know. But they were being a little -- I dunno -- Does seem a little funny...

RACHEL: Going on a trip -- Hope they don't get into the flood.

OLDTIMER: Yeah, me, too. If there IS a flood.

JUDE: There IS one. We're ALL going on a trip. [He stands up.] Thanks for the cake, Oldtimer. Pack up what you feel like carrying, and we'll go do the same. We'll be back for you in a little while. [To RACHEL] C'mon, Honey. We gotta get a move on.

RACHEL [She stands up. She and JUDE begin putting on raincoats.]: O.K., Jude. I wish we didn't have to go. It's frightening, and -- and, annoying.

OLDTIMER [He is sitting still, staring at them.]: You guys really leaving?

JUDE: We have to. And you need to pack, too.

OLDTIMER: I'm not going.

RACHEL: You're not?!

OLDTIMER: Nope.

RACHEL: Why not? Everyone has to evacuate!

OLDTIMER: Not me. They can't make me. And it's too much trouble. I don't believe there's gonna even be a flood. Just the sheriff pretending he's a big shot.

JUDE: I don't think so, Oldtimer. [He opens the door.] C'mon with us. You get your stuff together. We'll share -- we'll go it together -- the three of us.

OLDTIMER: I really appreciate your a bein' willing to bother with me -- really -- but I'll just stay.

RACHEL: Oh, no, Oldtimer. I'll worry about you.

OLDTIMER: I'll be all right. [Pause] Actually, I wish you wouldn't go.

JUDE: We have to. We'll stop by on our way. [They exit. JUDE's voice offstage] See you in a little. [OLDTIMER closes the door gently and shakes his head.]

Two

They always go. They come, but then they go.

Wish they wouldn't go, but they do.

They always go -- no matter who it is. They're really good people -- Rachel and Jude. Good neighbors. Never had kids. Real generous with me -- lookin' out for me, without bein' pushy.

Lemme sit and look at my cake. I hear talk that people are gettin' worse. I even hear people say that the human race is so bad -- "evil," they say, that's the word they like -- so evil that we all deserve killing. I can hardly imagine that. Hell, that would have to include THEM, wouldn't it? And it's so stupid. As if everybody was all bad, as bad as could be. Hell, I'm not particularly good -- far from perfect, I'd be the first to admit -- but I'm sure as hell not as bad as I coulda been! And there are lotsa decent people around.

They're all over -- just tryin' to figure out how to get through life. Like Jude and Rachel, there. They worry more'n what's good for a body. But they're fine people -- work hard, come check up on me --

Ha! Makin' sure I haven't croaked in the night, they are. Good neighbors. They take care of themselves, and if someone needs help, they're right there -- with no horn tooting and no big fuss.

Naw, people are O.K.. I LIKE people. Oh, I know there's rascals out there among 'em. Dangerous maniacs, even. No doubt about it. But most people aren't BAD.

The worst are the ones who think they're better'n other folks. My grandson's a little like that. Arrogant, you might say. The kind of people that make up lotsa rules and then think that they're exceptions, that the rules are for OTHER people. Causes more damn trouble.

Yeah, but I still like people -- for the most part.

There ARE two kinds that I try to stay clear of. One is the kind that expect other folks to take care of 'em -- gimme, gimme, gimme -- instead a gettin' out there and gettin' at it and takin' care of themselves. I mean, there are some that don't seem to be trying. Just -- SUCKING. And they'll suck you dry, if you let 'em.

Then there's the other kind -- so eager to help. They butt in, take over, if you let 'em -- help, help, help. Busybodies, they are. And actually they get in the way -- they interfere. Drive a body nuts. You finally hafta tell 'em to back away. "Quit bein' so goddam helpful! Let ME do it!"

'Course, if the titty-bottle suckers get together with the help-help-helpers, I guess that's O.K. -- I just want 'em to stay outa MY way. I mean, I'm busy. I have things to do, things to THINK about, for God's sake.

I'm responsible for me.

I mean, you have to take charge of your life. You have to run your own life.

Sometimes you get stuck. Life boxes you in. Something, circumstances, maybe, plugs things up. But you hafta break out. My third wife had a saying -- at the time I always thought it was too hard, but I've had time to think about it --

Now, there was a woman for you. Wise --

What a woman --

She used to say, "Let the dead bury the dead." It hardly made sense, at first. I used to argue with her, but she'd argue back -- "If you're gonna LIVE, you can't let yourself get stuck with folks who AREN'T, who aren't gonna live themselves and aren't gonna let YOU live!"

She was quite a woman --

I knew some old people -- elderly people, like me, let's say -- who always wanted someone to take care of 'em. I've watched 'em. They hop from Mama-Helper to Wife-Helper, to Daughter-Helper and maybe Granddaughter-Helper -- always being taken care of -- and they never have a time in there when they're taking care of themselves.

Well, I outlived all o' THEM. That sucking baby stage is miserable for everybody. But usually it's short, thank God. They don't live as long as I have. 'Course, I been busy. Seven wives. Always a garden. And family --

I was thinking the other day -- oh, sure, I keep busy THINKING! Just thinking. Trying to figure what the hell's goin' on! Came to something the other day. A fella has to learn to say, "No." Ya hafta learn to refuse. Babies do it. Often it's the first word they learn. "No!" I've watched 'em, sittin' on that rug there, waving a rattle, chanting, "No, no, no." Well, we go to a lot of trouble to train that out of 'em -- and the secret of a long and happy life is to learn all over again how to say it.

"NO!"

See? Has a ring to it doesn't it?

"NO! No-no!"

I finally learned it. Oh, you don't have to shout it. You have to DO it. Refuse. Refuse, if that's what you really want to do. Refuse to volunteer.

Refuse to lend.

Refuse to take on more projects.

Refuse to promise, especially if it's something stupid -- death bed promises are really -- I mean, REFUSE!

"Let the dead bury the dead."

Refuse to spend time with people who have made a fine art out of making you feel bad. Life's too short, I can tell you. And mine's been LONG!

God, that's a lotta rain.

I'm thinking, it takes a lotta guts to be old.

Not everyone makes it.

And not everyone makes it with everything intact. Teeth, hair, the mental stuff in here -- knock on wood.

I'm thankful for my -- well, my MIND. My memories -- I spend a lot of time with them -- and my horse sense. Oh, I still got it -- I can still put two and two together.

My sixth wife was almost as old as I was. What a woman --

She'd say, "Senility is the mercy shown to those who can't stand retrospection." I used to argue with HER, too, that that was too harsh. I mean, sometimes senility is loneliness, or malnutrition, or brain damage caused by medicine -- I don't know. Anyway it's scary for old folks -- I should know. I'm just glad I'm -- all HERE!

What was I talking about?

I had an idea, but it got away, and I haven't got it back, yet.

Hmm-hmmm.

Well, it'll come.

Ha! Notice how that little word, "yet," changes things. "I haven't got it back, YET." Makes it positive. I will get it back, but not enough time has gone by, not enough patience has been learned, something hasn't ripened enough, or something -- yet. And "yet" applies to everything, in this kind of a world.

"He hasn't come back, yet."

"She hasn't been kissed, yet."

"He hasn't been caught, yet."

"She hasn't been paid, yet."

"He's never won, yet."

"She's never lost, yet."

Ha! THERE it is! That idea that I mislaid. Yeah! It's tough being old, what with senility and God knows what all else to look out for -- but there are priveleges that go with being old. For one thing, old folks can say what they really think. And that's a great relief, really.

I remember when I turned four hundred -- my father had already died, I guess -- my grandfather was the one that raised me, really -- I remember kinda DECIDING, or realizing anyway, that I didn't have to defer to my elders anymore. After a certain point, you don't really HAVE elders anymore. You're one of 'em, and you're all the same -- more or less equal, merely OLD, and hopefully wise -- but anyway, you can say what you think. If it's too outlandish, they'll say, "Oldtimer's getting senile!" But you don't have to hold it in. It can GET SAID.

But there's another side to THAT, too. Some folks -- and not always old folks, when I think about it, but often it's old folks -- think they've been "enlightened."

Ha-ha. They think there's a stage you can get to which they call -- "Enlightenment." And they're always hinting at the fact that they're enlightened and other folks aren't. I tell 'em -- well, it was really that sixth wife of mine usedta tell 'em --

What a woman!

"There's no such thing as 'Enlightenment'!" I came to agree with her. Those Great Enlightened Marvels are phoneys, frauds. They're not enlightened. They're befuddled. There's no such thing.

Oh, I think we can find out things. In fact, that's what I think we oughta be doing. Fitting pieces together. Oh. Just so! Yes! I see. Thusly! That is a kind of enlightenment. Some little thing is figured out. The Whole Thing --

That's something else. I think The Whole Thing is too big to figure out. "Problem solving" is fine. And "thinking clearly" is fine, too. Old folks oughta be busy doing both things. But "Enlightenment," like a finished process -- naw, that's my grandson's department. Not for me.

My God, that's a lotta rain. The most I EVER remember.

You live a while and pay attention all the while, and you get to see a lot of things come and go. One garden after another. They become hard to keep track of in your mind. Wives. I've had seven. Kings, tribes, republics, empires -- lots of 'em come and go. All kinds of crazy projects -- walls, pyramids, ziggurats, temples, armadas -- people find the damnedest things to live and die for. Keep your wits about you, and watch it all come and go -- and you DO get wiser.

I don't believe it, really, but I can see why some folks are saying that the human race is getting worse. There's more of us, for one thing. We're more crowded. Cities are the worst. And the empires suck up everything -- and more and more people are afraid of living and scared of dying --

What!? Oh --

OLDTIMER [Startled at first by a loud knock on the door]: That'll be Jude and Rachel. [He jumps up eagerly and opens the door.] C'mon in!

JUDE [Voice outside, as RACHEL enters]: You ready? [JUDE enters. He and RACHEL are burdened with backpacks under clear plastic sheeting. They carry hiking sticks. RACHEL has on muddy four-buckle arctic boots. JUDE is wearing hip boots rolled down to his knees and is carrying an old small empty army knapsack.]

RACHEL [To OLDTIMER]: You DIDN'T pack.

OLDTIMER: Naw. I'm not going.

RACHEL: Everybody's supposed to evacuate, Oldtimer.

JUDE: And there IS flooding. The river's backed up. Ditches are overflowing. Look! [He crosses to the window and points out. OLDTIMER follows him to the window.] See!

OLDTIMER: Oh-oh. My garden IS getting an early irrigation.

RACHEL: It's a mess. C'mon. Get yourself ready, Oldtimer. We gotta get going.

OLDTIMER: Naw --

RACHEL: Everybody's going.

JUDE: Sheriff's Department is going house to house.

OLDTIMER: Let 'em.

RACHEL [Pacing, fretting]: We'll probably lose everything.

OLDTIMER [Quoting a proverb]: "More was lost in the Fire!"

RACHEL: I mean, what'll be left here when we get back? [She stops. To OLDTIMER] WHAT fire?

OLDTIMER [Scratching his head]: I dunno. It was something my father always said when somebody complained about losing something. [He quotes it again.] "More was lost in the FIRE!"

JUDE: I didn't know you knew your father.

OLDTIMER: Oh, yeah. [Musing. RACHEL is impatient.] He was a strange one. Downright weird. Wonder what the hell fire he meant.

RACHEL: It doesn't matter. We'll just be lucky if anything's here when we get back. I mean, adobe houses in a flood like this --

JUDE: We can just be glad, after all, that we don't have little kids.

RACHEL [Putting her hands to her cheeks and wailing]: Ohh!!

OLDTIMER [Putting an arm around her, wanting to console her]: Now, now, Rachel. Don't fret so. You guys go on -- and I'll just stay and look after things here.

RACHEL: We'll lose everything.

OLDTIMER: Maybe -- [He looks at her.] My second wife used to say -- [He squeezes RACHEL's shoulders a little.] Now, there was a woman -- [He muses, remembering.] What a woman --

JUDE: What did she say? And we better get going.

OLDTIMER: She said often, I remember -- [He quotes.] "Life doesn't add up to all the stuff we accumulate." Used to say it especially when she was cleaning out some storage place and throwing trash away.

RACHEL: Well, what DOES life add up to?

OLDTIMER [Caught short, momentarily]: Uh -- well, let's see -- it adds up to -- [He lets go of RACHEL and scratches his head.] It adds up to -- hugs like that, and memories, and -- wisdom -- and years.

JUDE: Yeah, and you've got lots of all o' that, eh, Oldtimer?

OLDTIMER: I sure do.

JUDE: How many years?

OLDTIMER: I'll never tell.

RACHEL [Hugging OLDTIMER, a little desperately]: Happy Birthday, Oldtimer. You've been a wonderful neighbor. I hope you'll be safe.

OLDTIMER [Patting her shoulder in the embrace]: Oh, I'll be all right. YOU be careful, traipsing off to the mountains in the rain.

RACHEL: Everyone's supposed to go --

OLDTIMER: I know. But I'm a stubborn old geezer.

JUDE: How old?

OLDTIMER: Never mind. [He lets go of RACHEL and shakes hands with JUDE.]

JUDE: Think you can handle it?

OLDTIMER: Sure.

JUDE: I worry about these mud houses, in rain and flood --

OLDTIMER: This old house is gonna be fine. I'll be all right.

JUDE: We'll go, then. [He opens the door.]

OLDTIMER: You can't stay for another piece of birthday cake?

JUDE: No. We better be going.

RACHEL [To OLDTIMER]: Be sure and give me the recipe when we get back.

OLDTIMER: I sure will. See you later. [They exit.] 'Bye!

JUDE [Voice offstage]: So long, Oldtimer.

RACHEL [Voice offstage]: We love you, Oldtimer. Thanks for everything! Goodbye!

OLDTIMER: 'Bye! [He stands in the open door and waves. He watches them go and then studies the irrigation of his garden.] That IS a lot of water. Hope they'll be all right. "We love you," she says. [Shouts after them.] I love you, too! [He closes the door. He goes to the window and looks out. He studies the sky. It is still raining.]

Three

Love, she says. They leave, and you're still alive.

Cake looks lonely there. Almost silly.

Jude sure was curious about my age. But I didn't want any more of that argument. People think I'm kidding, or out of my mind -- you know, SENILE! So I quit telling.

Longevity runs in my family. My grandfather Jared died two hundred thirty years ago at the ripe old age of nine hundred sixty-two. HIS father lived to be eight hundred ninety-five. My son, Lamech, died just five years ago, two years after I passed Grandfather Jared's world record. Lamech was only seven hundred seventy-seven.

Let's see, now. Nine hundred sixty-TWO plus TWO plus FIVE -- that makes this my nine hundred sixty-ninth birthday! Can you imagine that many candles, or that many pancakes?

But it's better not to tell. You tell people, "Come on over and have a hunk o' my nine hundred sixty-ninth birthday cake," and they look at you funny, and cock their heads, and walk around you looking at you, and think to themselves and maybe even say out loud as if you were deaf -- "That old bastard's positively senile!" So I don't tell 'em any more.

My father, Enoch, was a strange duck. My grandson reminds me o' him.

I remember -- a regular weirdo, my father was. Heard voices. Always building altars and shrines -- and he really seemed to believe that stuff. He disappeared at the age of three hundred sixty-five.

Ha! One year for every day in the year. I never noticed or thought of that before.

Anyway, he just disappeared. We never knew if he ran off, or died somewhere, drowned in a ditch, maybe -- or whether there was foul play -- I was only three hundred when he vanished, and no one ever saw him again.

'Course, if he's still living, somewhere -- and I guess he might be -- he'd be the oldest now, instead a me.

Numbers are funny. Sometimes I wonder what they're for. I mean, what needs counting?

Count your money? Ha! What's it good for? Won't make the garden grow. Won't make someone love you. Oh, people think it might, but it won't. Won't make it stop raining.

My fourth wife's father --

Now, SHE was quite a woman -- But her father --

What a woman --

Her old man used to count his accounts receivable. People owed him money, he said. They never paid it, that I ever knew of. They may not even've thought they owed it, for all I could tell, but he used to make little notations on adobe bricks, and count THEM. I always told him it was like counting the eggs under a settin' hen as if they were chickens -- insteada bein' surprised at the miracle when one hatched.

Well, I use the numbers to count years. In fact, it's interesting to see who counts winters and who counts summers. "He's been through two hundred winters." That's a pessimist. Winter is hard on you and wears you out, so the more you've been through, the nearer you are to the end, I guess.

"She's seen six hundred summers." It's positive. Sunshine, gardens, warm nights.

Mmm-MMM. I love warm nights.

Years can be hard to keep track of. The year the pump froze. The year the cow had twins. The year my first wife died. Now, there was a woman --

What a woman --

The year Shem was drafted. The year the war ended. I number 'em. I've decided that's what numbers are for.

Nine hundred sixty-nine.

Even with the numbers they all begin to get mushed together and feel more and more alike.

It's bad enough when you're young. I mean you tell me the difference between sixty-two and sixty-three. Oh, I know, when you're REALLY young, it does make a difference. Three is very much different from four. And twelve is very much different from thirteen. But --

I really can't tell you the difference between nine hundred eight and nine hundred nine --

My son Lamech wasn't much into numbers. I tried to interest him in all that, but he'd get up and walk out and go hoe the garden. He never cared about numbers. Maybe because I DID!

I felt bad about Lamech there for a while. I mean, can you imagine getting to be seven hundred years old, and your old man's still living?

Weaning is a very important process, for both parties. I tried to cut him loose, without bein' mean about it, but I was never sure he quite made it. I used to tell him, "If you hear a little voice inside you saying, 'You're not all right. That's not good enough. There's something the matter with you,' and you can't figure out what the hell -- then that's ME, Lamech, your old man, inside you. Me, when I was younger and stupid. Forget it. Ignore it. Laugh at it. Don't fight ME, now, and don't sulk -- just get rid of it -- that stupid little voice."

But I was never sure he got it. He died five years ago.

God, that's a lotta rain. And look at the mess in that garden. Half under water. "That's enough, You Guys! Garden's got a good drink, and then some. No need to wash all the good soil AWAY.

I guess you might say I've learned to take things as they come. This'll be the year it rained one helluva lot.

But there's no use getting all lathered up about things. I learned that, quite a while ago. You can't change things, and you can't keep things from changing.

But, hell, you can't get to be nine hundred sixty-nine years old and not be a nice guy. Mellow, y'know. Laid back. Meanness kills you off early. Oh, I went through a dangerous period there -- about the time my father ran off --

If that's what he did. Just disappeared. We didn't know what to do, where to look, whether to look --

I spent too much energy, mean energy, piling up stuff and trying to BE somebody.

Hell, you ARE somebody, I said to myself one day. EVERYbody's SOMEbody. And you don't have to grab the other guy's stuff, or even worry about your own THAT much. Enjoy the ride. Life's a ride. Merrily we roll along. Enjoy it.

I made a list once. All the things life is.

"Life is a dream."

And when do we wake up? Ha-ha.

"Life is a bowl of cherries."

"Life is a test, and this quiz counts, Kid."

"Life is, at best, a grim and relentless struggle."

"Life is a pain where you can't put a plaster."

"Life is a shit sandwich and we're out of bread."

Damn pessimists got nasty with that one, didn't they?

"Life is just one damn thing after another."

Ain't it the truth?

"Life is a jigsaw puzzle, and no one guy has all the pieces."

That one's for my grandson -- he's always so damn SURE.

"Life is a maze we'll never get out of alive."

Ha! "All of the above!"

Ha! "None of the above!"

I wonder about gettin' out of here alive. Sometimes I almost think I can't die. I had some close calls early on -- everybody does. Was drafted, but lived through that somehow. Fell out of the cherry tree once. Cut myself with the sickle -- got quite a scar, here.

But you get to be my age -- I feel good. I eat well. Everything works -- just fine. I'm curious about the world. I like people. I enjoy being here. I don't get all bent outa shape by whatever happens -- and sometimes I wonder if I'm immune --

Hey! I discovered the cure for the common cold. Yeah. Really! Don't GET one!

All that talk about not getting your feet wet -- actually, it's quite a day for that out there. And, don't get caught in a draft. Or, don't allow yourself to be sneezed on. Eat lots of oranges and garlic -- all that helps, I suppose, but I used to tell Lamech, the best thing is to decide not to. "Be busy. Too busy enjoying living. And if you need to take a day off, TAKE it. Don't make yourself sick with a cold first, so you'll have an excuse to take off. You get a day off with a cold, and you have to spend it being miserable."

People don't believe it's that simple. I told my grandson, "If you think this is the kind of world in which Something is out to get you, to punish you -- and it doesn't matter what name you give to that 'Something' -- you'll have lots of colds. They'll be common." 'Course, he thinks I'm a senile old man --

Wonder what the hell trip that was they were going on?

My second wife and I discovered this cure for the common cold. Love your body -- all of it, every aspect of it -- and each other's --

What a woman SHE was --

Take care of it. Use it for your daily work. Exercise

it. Walking is excellent. Gardening is good. Swimming also, although we don't usually do much swimming in this desert.

Plenty of swimming holes out there at the moment. Poor garden. It'll take some work to put it back together now. Floods always wreck the ditch system.

But the neighbors will all help. Gardens are good for co-operation. Patience and sharing. And maybe a little flooding will be a good thing. Bring in new soil, in exchange for what's being washed away.

[Two young uniformed rescue squad workers, ZEKE and ALETHA, appear at the window in a rowboat. ZEKE is rowing.]

ALETHA [Calling, with her hands on the windowsill]: Anybody in there?

OLDTIMER [Startled severely]: What the hell --? [He sees ALETHA.] Where'd YOU come from?

ZEKE: Never mind. Let's go.

ALETHA [To ZEKE]: We hafta pick him up.

ZEKE: We can't! This damn boat --

ALETHA: It's our job, Zeke. [Climbing in the window] I'll get him --

OLDTIMER [Backing away]: Get me?

ALETHA: C'mon, Oldtimer. We gotta go.

OLDTIMER [Still backing away from her]: Go where?

ALETHA: To the mountains.

ZEKE [Still in the rowboat, calling in the window to ALETHA]: If he doesn't wanta go, leave him, and let's US go.

ALETHA [To OLDTIMER]: C'mon. The Fire Department is evacuating everybody.

OLDTIMER: Why?

ZEKE: There's no time to talk about it.

ALETHA [To OLDTIMER]: The seacoast cities are gone -- underwater. Miami and Montevideo and Marseilles and Manila --

OLDTIMER: Really?

ZEKE: Let's GO!

ALETHA: The rivers aren't flowing.

OLDTIMER: I noticed ours has backed up.

ALETHA: River cities are now under new lakes. Memphis, Madrid, Moscow.

ZEKE [To ALETHA]: Quit blatherin' and grab him, if you insist on bringin' him.

ALETHA [To ZEKE]: It usually works better if people understand what's happening to them.

ZEKE: Who understands this goddam flood! It's the end of the world!

OLDTIMER [To ALETHA]: Is it the end of the world?

ALETHA: It's a bad flood. C'mon. [She takes his arm and they go to the window.]

OLDTIMER: I just up and go with you?

ALETHA: Yes. C'mon.

OLDTIMER [To ALETHA]: What's your name?

ZEKE: We don't have time for formal introductions!

OLDTIMER [To ALETHA]: His name is Zeke-in-a-hurry. What's yours?

ALETHA: Aletha.

OLDTIMER [After letting it register]: Good name. [He looks out the window into the rowboat. To ZEKE] Your boat's leaking.

ZEKE: I know it is.

OLDTIMER: Can't the county provide you guys with boats that don't leak?

ALETHA: It was fine, until Zeke --

ZEKE [Interrupting]: We're going, Oldtimer. Are you coming or not?

OLDTIMER: You're not going very far in that. And if I get in, we'll ALL sink! I know my boats, better'n you do, it looks like.

ALETHA: C'mon, Oldtimer. [She tries to lift him, but he jumps away from the window.]

OLDTIMER: Aletha, Honey, that boat isn't safe. I'm better off here -- and you would be, too. Stay here, and let old Zeke-in-a-hurry go to the mountains.

ALETHA: I have work to do, Oldtimer. [She climbs out the window.] You're not coming?

OLDTIMER: Nope.

ALETHA: What do you know about your grandson?

OLDTIMER: Noah?

ALETHA: His place is deserted.

OLDTIMER: They went on a trip a week ago.

ALETHA: Oh, good. And the neighbors downstream?

OLDTIMER: Jude and Rachel? They left walking. Early this morning. They may need help. But you can't help anybody with THAT boat.

ZEKE [To ALETHA]: Let's GO!

ALETHA [To ZEKE]: O.K. Be careful you don't punch any more holes in the bottom.

ZEKE: You let me worry about that. [He pushes away from the house with an oar at the window. OLDTIMER hops to the window.]

OLDTIMER [Calling as they slide out of sight]: You'd do better to fix your boat, and THEN try to help people! [He waves.] 'Bye, Aletha. Thanks for -- [Quieter] caring -- about an old man. [He stares after them, and then turns finally back into the room.]

Four

Now, there's the Fire Department -- people trying to help each other. Serious about their work, even though they're slightly outa their usual element. But they're trying. Wonder how far they'll get. Outa sight already.

Hell, they don't need to bother with ME. There must be lotsa kids around that need rescuing. I don't wanta go with them anyway. Terrified Zeke hardly knows what he's doing.

Aletha was nice. Really nice. Hmm -- too young for someone MY age, I suppose.

But I been thinkin', I need to find me somebody. Yeah. Somebody to love. My grandson said, not long ago, "You mean seven wives weren't enough?"

I told him, "Listen, Young Fella, while it lasts, it's good! And when you're OLD, it's good. All the better, in fact. And I can't waste this -- this, whatever it is -- being loyal to a dead person. I need to find a live one and be loyal to HER -- and, and be ALIVE!"

He was scandalized. So I just tease him all the more.

Oh! His kids were singin' a song the other day -- I don't always pay attention to the words the kids are singin' -- you know how that is. But, get this.

"Kiss me, my sweet. And so let us part. And when I grow too old to dream --"

"What?" I yelled, interrupting the kids' singing. "Too old to -- WHAT?"

"Too old to dream," they said.

"Dream!" I yelled. "You mean ACT. Too old to PERFORM. To DO something."

Kids thought the old man was nuts, I'm sure. But I raved on. "What a quitter! Dream! And DO! And when you can't do, you go on dreaming. That never ends. If you can imagine getting too old to dream, you've already quit dreaming -- and you're ALREADY too old to dream -- too old to do anything -- and so why should I kiss you, you old fart! Scram! None of this and-so-let-us-part crap. Get lost!" Kids scratched their heads and looked at each other and went outside to hoe the garden.

People ASSUME that old folks have lost their -- uh, faculties. And maybe some have, and many some haven't, and maybe some faculties and not others.

Yeah. They call me a dirty old man. I know. But I don't care.

"Standin' on the corner, watchin' all the girls go by --"

Clothes are a funny business. You stand there on the corner, or in the garden, or in your own house, and -- use your imagination. Who would you like to see -- stripped? I used to talk like this with my grandson, and he'd get really upset. Said the whole imagination of my heart was only evil continually.

Ha! That's quite a mouthful to say about somebody. And who's he kidding? And who's gonna be offended? Hell, if you ask me, it'd be a lot more offensive to a woman, if she ever found out that Mr. So-and-so did NOT strip her in his imagination. Found her THAT unattractive, clothes and all. Had THAT little curiosity about her.

What started all this?

Oh, yes. Having that delicious Aletha climb in my window. She was a very nice lady.

And I need somebody like that to love. Yes, I'd marry again. Probably will, when we get this flood over with. I'll sure be on the look-out.

My grandson says when two people marry, they become ONE. I tell him I don't think that's the best way to put it. Marriage is an agreement to change from two solos to a duet. Not that you're gonna BE one thing instead of two. You're gonna be two people DOING one thing. Changes the whole feel of it. Makes ya humble. Just imagine, she's willing to take part in a duet with me. I mean, it's really quite an honor to be asked to be the other half of a duet.

But who wants a nine-hundred-sixty-nine-year-old man? "Be realistic." That's what my grandson would say.

He didn't even wanta take me on his little trip.

He's a funny duck. Thinks he has a special hotline to the Source, or something. Lets that crazy notion run his life -- and he ends up thinking he's better'n other people. And HE has problems.

He has a drinking problem, for one.

He thinks his name means something special. My first wife named him, six hundred years ago. Said it meant "relief," in her language. Relief. Hmp, not much relief, I'd say.

Zeke used a phrase that Noah usedta love. "The End of the World." Noah worries about people having fun.

"Life is a test." And for my grandson, if you enjoyed yourself, you failed. So he goes around, NOT enjoying himself much and hindering other folks' enjoyment as much as he can. Not curious, not friendly, not loving, not living.

Oh, well, I don't know why I'm thinking of HIM so much. He's away on a trip, and we're having a flood. His place'll be a wreck, too, when he gets back. I guess I just really don't like the signal that he keeps sending out, that he thinks he's better'n other people. That arrogance of his is so stupid. Hell, you live long enough, and be honest about it, and you know damn well no one is any better'n anyone else. We're different, that's all. And I LIKE THE DIFFERENCES! Mostly.

The end of the world. Hmm -- that's a lotta water. The most I've ever seen, except at the ocean. Never thought I'd see it here.

Noah says the world is made of water. I argued with him once about it. I said I thought it was made of fire. I can feel a fire in my belly, here.

Sometimes, I feel a fire in my bones. The sun is a huge fire ball. I think the stars are, too -- like campfires on a mountainside when you're a day's hike away. The earth is afire underneath -- I saw those volcanoes in action over by the Dead Sea, long before Noah was born. It's fire, all right.

But he said, "No, it's water. The Creator/Source, who speaks to me, made it all out of water, and divided the water from above beyond where the stars are, from the water beneath the earth. He pushed the Chaos back, and made a world."

I can just hear him now -- "And when he decides to, he'll unmake the world. He'll turn it back into water. He'll open the windows of heaven, and the fountains of the great deep shall burst forth --"

Not a bad description of what's happening out there, really! It's a watery chaos.

Chaos. Fire and water. Ice. Big bangs and whimpers -- Hell, that's all crazy.

"The End of the World." The Whole Thing can't end. It just goes on and on. Our little world is not the whole -- World! He doesn't think big enough and longtime enough.

It's a wonder there's a world at all, for one thing. I mean, it doesn't have to be the way it is. It just is. This time. Maybe it wasn't once and maybe it won't be again, and it's a safe bet that it never has been this way before. But it goes on being and not being, all the different ways it can.

Ha! Noah hated that kind of talk. He always wanted it so he could BLAME somebody for -- whatever. He said his Source/Creator -- whatever he called it -- was angry!

Now that's a real puzzlement. Made a world, and then was angry at it. As if that made any sense at all! I asked him, "What's he mad at?"

Noah said, "At humanity."

"What for?" I asked.

"They are evil," he said.

"And who made 'em that way, if they are?" I argued.

He couldn't answer. But he had his head full of all kinds of crazy stuff like that.

Hmm. Raining harder than ever out there, and the wind's up.

That Creator of Noah's doesn't like curious, busy, experimenters with life. Enjoyers. Lovers. Livers. He'd like to hinder you from doing things and finding out things.

Mmm. Good cake, even if I made it and say so myself.

"Yield not to temptation," Noah'd say.

And I'd tease him, "I'm too old for temptation." Mmm. I'm not, though. Thank God. Good cake. I teased Noah too much, maybe. "The spirit is willing," I'd tell him, "but the flesh is BUSY!" Ha! Ha-ha. Poor guy. I gave him a hard time.

[The rowboat with ZEKE and ALETHA returns to the window. OLDTIMER watches them approach.]

OLDTIMER: Well, hello! [He's glad to see ALETHA and continually eyes her up and down.] Welcome back. C'mon in. [He takes ALETHA's hand and helps her in the window.]

ALETHA: You must come now, Oldtimer. Immediately.

ZEKE: No stalling to discuss it.

OLDTIMER: What's the hurry?

ALETHA: The mountains have become islands. Moriah. Matterhorn. McKinley.

OLDTIMER: So what'll happen at OUR mountains? What'll people live on?

ALETHA: It's our only chance. [She takes his elbow.] C'mon.

ZEKE [Terrified, verging on hysteria]: All flesh is dying. Cattle. Birds. Snakes, even. [He points out on the water.] Look! We've found dead bodies floating. The world is beginning to stink.

OLDTIMER [To ALETHA]: Is he all right?

ALETHA: Not really.

ZEKE: The drinking water is gone. All springs and wells are befouled. Water, water everywhere -- and not a drop to drink.

OLDTIMER [Laughing]: Is he putting on an act?

ALETHA: No, Oldtimer. He isn't. C'mon.

ZEKE [To OLDTIMER, as a chant]: What is your name?

ALETHA [Greatly puzzled, to ZEKE]: What does that matter? I thought you were in a hurry.

ZEKE [Almost in a trance, to OLDTIMER]: What is your name?

OLDTIMER: They call me Oldtimer. [Musing, quieter] But I DO have a name. No one uses it any more. Too many years old to need a name.

ALETHA [Genuinely interested -- there IS a spark between her and OLDTIMER, to OLDTIMER]: What IS your name?

OLDTIMER: Methusaleh. [Long pause. To ZEKE] But I'm just a very old man, Zeke. You go along and rescue some younger people. There must be some around here. [To ALETHA] And you stay keep me company here. We'll have a good time, and when this is over --

ALETHA: I can't stay, Oldtimer. And you can't either. Your house is about to dissolve. We'd put you on the roof, but it won't last long enough to make it worth the bother. So, c'mon --

OLDTIMER: No. You should stay. [He points at ZEKE.] HE'LL be the death of you.

ALETHA: Why are you so stubborn?

OLDTIMER: I want to go on living.

ZEKE [Sounding like part of a chant]: The world is no fit place for anyone to live in.

OLDTIMER: I have work to do. And things to learn.

ALETHA: If you want to go on living -- [She raises OLDTIMER's arm to the window sill.]

ZEKE [Chanting, almost in shock]: WHY go on living? There is no reason, no purpose --

OLDTIMER [A little sharply]: Being alive is better than being dead.

ZEKE: Is it?

OLDTIMER: Yes, it is. [To ZEKE] YOU'RE dead already! How are YOU gonna rescue anybody? [To ALETHA] You shouldn't go with him. Really. Stay here, where it's safe. [He takes hold of HER elbow.]

ZEKE [Chanting]: There is no place safe.

OLDTIMER [To ZEKE]: Oh, shut up! You make me sick! [To ALETHA] Please, stay.

ALETHA: You're not afraid, Oldtimer?

OLDTIMER: Afraid of what?

ZEKE [Chanting]: It is the end of the world.

OLDTIMER [To ZEKE]: You shut up!

ALETHA [To OLDTIMER]: It may be the end of all of US.

OLDTIMER: It may be. That's no reason to do something stupid. [He looks at the leaking boat-bottom, then at the new storm. The wind is rising.] No reason to get into a sinking boat. [He puts his hand on ALETHA's arm.] And I'm glad of one thing.

ALETHA: Glad! What is there to be glad of?

ZEKE [Chanting]: The end of the world ...

OLDTIMER: At least it's not some man-made disaster.

ALETHA: Man-made...

ZEKE [Chanting]: The end of the world ...

OLDTIMER: All the wars. That last war -- [He stops. Muses long, looking off, remembering. Quoting] "More was lost in the Fire!" [He pauses, while ALETHA stares at his face.] My father said it was a huge man-made fire. [Back to ALETHA] This is better. A person somehow doesn't mind earthquakes and sabre-toothed tigers. And floods. [More animated] They're a challenge. Almost like part of the deal. "Let's see your guts," the world is saying. [He looks askance at ZEKE. Quieter] Poor bastard. [Very quietly, to ALETHA] Stay with me.

ALETHA [Climbing out the window into the rowboat]: I can't. [She turns back.] I'd like to. Really, Oldtimer, I'd like to. I like you. I'd be glad -- [She stops and stares into his face.] But Duty calls. I can't quit. Not yet.

OLDTIMER [Holding her arm, as she holds the windowsill]: You're not gonna get anywhere in that sinking boat.

ALETHA: Maybe not. But I gotta try.

OLDTIMER [To ALETHA]: Stay. We could -- do a fine duet together.

ALETHA: I can't. Let me go.

OLDTIMER: Wait. [Urgently] Wait! [He turns and runs to his table, picks up what's left of his birthday cake and brings it to the window.] Here. It's my birthday. Take what's left of my cake. I've had enough.

ALETHA [Letting go of the windowsill to take the cake]: Your birthday? [The boat begins to float her and ZEKE away.] Oh, Oldtimer.

ZEKE [Chanting]: It's the end of the world ...

ALETHA [From offstage]: Goodbye, Oldtimer. Thanks for asking me. [Urgently] I'll look you up, later! [Her voice fades in more storm.] Bye! Good-bye!

OLDTIMER [Waving at the window] Bye! Good-bye, Aletha. [He stays long at the window, trying to keep track of them. At last he turns back into the room and kicks a stool violently.] How far can they get? [He feels sorry for himself.] Everything goes. Everything goes away. [The storm rages and the rain pours.]

Five

"The end of the world." They come and they go.

"The end of the world."

"There is no place safe. The end of the world."

Just about the time I get myself convinced that I'm an exception -- that I can skip the end, just go on past the end, and keep right on going, with NO end -- we have the Noah Memorial End of the World. No exceptions. No exceptions?!

Hey, out there! I'm an exception!

Don't you ignore me! You can't do this to me! It's my birthday!

Nine hundred sixty-nine. As if the numbers mattered...

Everyone gets a turn, finally.

I remember as a little kid how hard it was for me to wait for my turn. "Is it my turn yet?"

"Whose turn is it?"

"It takes so long for it to get to be my turn!"

"Can I play? Let me in the game, Coach."

Hm. So, now it's my turn, after all. At long last, I get to play. This is gonna be it.

"But I wanta be a liver."

"Hey, hear this, you guys. Kid says he wants to be a liver."

"Well, what's wrong with that? So he wants to be liver. Hell, I'd rather be a pancrease myself, but if he wants to be a liver, it's O.K. by me."

"Go ahead, Kid. Be a liver. It won't bother me none. Live it up."

And now it gets to be my turn to be a die-er.

[OLDTIMER goes slowly to the trunk against the wall and very slowly opens it. He pulls out sacks of coins and sets them on the floor. He rummages through clothing.]

OLDTIMER: May as well dress for the occasion. [He rummages some more.]

Here it is [He stands and takes his shirt off. He pulls from the trunk a bright white shirt with a huge brightly colored rainbow embroidered across the back. He starts to put it on over his head.]

My wife made me this ... [He stops midway, and then pokes his head out the neck opening.]

Now there was a woman! [He holds it thus, remembering. Then he finishes putting on the shirt.]

My turn, coming right up. [The storm rages.]

Well, I had my turn as a liver. Tried to enjoy life while it was happening. No use changing that now. Enjoy what is happening, Oldtimer. [He glances at the window.]

So it's raining. Desert people like to see it rain. Friendly interesting visitors come and go. I love 'em all. A chance to think. I mean, serious issues, heavy thoughts, no shortage of important things to think about. [He turns around, showing off the shirt.]

So, celebrate! [He sits at the table. He picks up cake crumbs with his fingers and eats them.]

In all those nine hundred sixty-nine years, I never tried running away. Never tried evacuating. Or being a refugee, just 'cause the county sheriff says so. [He pauses, thinking.]

I guess I really don't wanta try those things. Hiding from life. Ducking. No, I'll just keep on taking what it dishes out. [He brightens considerably.]

My grandfather Jared said something near the end of his very long life ... [He interrupts himself.]

Y'know, it pays to listen to old folks. They know things, and you never know when what they tell you will come in handy ... [He pauses, remembering.]

He said to me, "If you've really enjoyed life, tasted it all, drunk deep, every drop of all the juice, then Death itself will taste good." [Long pause.]

I used to think it would be best to let Something, whatever it is, interrupt me. Be busy doing my work, and it's never done, so keep at it, and let Whatever-It-Is interrupt me. Better not to think about it, maybe. [Long pause. He looks around the room a little lost.]

But what's to do, now? I'm all alone. Can't work the garden in the rain. The Flood is going to take away everything. So, if Something is gonna interrupt me, it'll have to be my thinking. Thinking like this. [The storm rages more violently. Oldtimer turns and looks out the window.]

My turn, coming right up. [Pause]

So think about it, Oldtimer. [Pause]

What happens to ya? [Pause. He looks at the clouds and then closes his eyes.]

Who knows? [He looks around the room.]

No one is gonna explain it to me. Not now. [He sits up straighter on his stool.]

So, let's see. [He gets ready to count on his fingers.]

Try and think clearly, Oldtimer. [The storm rages.]

What happens to ya when you die? [He counts a finger.]

One. Nothin' happens to ya. It's the end. You're through. Blotto. Lights out. [He makes quotation makes in the air.]

"The End." [He ponders, then shrugs his shoulders. He counts again.]

Two. Something bad happens to ya. That's where Noah is, I think. He lives scared, except when he's drunk. And goes around threatening other people. [He makes a face and shakes his head "no." Thunder crashes.]

I still don't think there's Someone angry, out there. [He counts again.]

Three. Something good happens to ya. [He shrugs again.]

That's obviously what we all want, but can't be sure of. We all act as if we didn't quite believe it. [He grins.]

Including me. [The storm rages. Oldtimer addresses the window.]

Take it easy, You Guys. [He returns to his fingers.]

Let's see, one, two, three. I'm not sure we are getting anywhere. It's a little hard to think, and a little late, maybe. Uh, there's a lot at stake, I mean, and it's really rough and noisy out there. [He counts.]

Four. You come back and try again and hope to do better next time, until you are -- [He makes quotation marks again.]

"Perfect." [He quotes Someone.]

"Tell me, Methusaleh, how'd you like to reach Perfection and be excused from further participation in the ceaseless and pointless round?" [Pause. He quotes his answer.]

"Naw, I don't wanta get to the point where I can't be improved upon and thus find myself deprived of the chance to come back and enjoy it all again." [Pause, then still quoting himself.]

"Yet." [Normal voice]

I sure as hell wouldn't wanta reach Perfection. That's the same as Blotto. [Pause, thinking hard.]

Who knows? [Pause, quizzically.]

How do ya find out? [A realization strikes him. Fear and courage and good humor combine in him.]

I'm about to find out! [He shakes his hands, getting rid of his categories.]

So it doesn't matter what people think about it, or what I guess about it in advance. [He stands up.]

I do believe one thing about it. I believe something just happens to ya. The Whole Thing. [He extends both arms, waving them.]

The Whole Thing is fair, whatever else it is. [Louder]

So be it! Whatever it is. [Pause]

I'll take it. [He shoots into the storm.]

Yes! I'll take it! [He comes back to his table and sits. Quietly, in a lull in the storm.]

It'll be as good as life was. [He touches the crumbs. He eats one.]

Good cake. Good life. And I'm about to find out. [He goes to the window and faces out so we can see his back and the rainbow on his shirt. The storm rages. In a lull.]

Who knows? [Thunder crashes. The light darkens. Rain pours. Surf roars nearby. In a lull, in a determined and excited voice.]

I'm about to find out. [Storm, thunder, surf, wind, water, rushing and roaring. The light darkens to grey, almost black. The light becomes blue, dark, deep blue. The storm subsides to absolute silence. The light brightens slightly in blue, showing the rainbow shirt in the underwater rapture. Then the light darkens, darker and darker, to black.]

SABOTAGE

Gibb's fellow-philosopher and life companion was out of town for the week-end, so his visit to the restaurant was intended to provide no more than physical nourishment, with a brief time to sit still. When left alone, he often found himself engaged in non-stop activity, not always fruitful, sometimes bordering on the frenetic. So he went to eat, and sit quietly, but he couldn't help overhearing the conversation in the next booth.

"... hook 'em together, multiply the power output." "... in the trunks of cars."

"... on Manny's flatbed. Just drive around town with the power on."

"... make him turn that copulating radio down, so he doesn't arouse suspicion and get caught."

Gibb went to the restroom, so he could get a good look at the occupants of that booth on his way back. Three young men, of assorted skin coloration, not fancily dressed, but not homeless and unwashed either. Earnest, serious. He paused in front of their booth, and they all glowered up at him in silence.

"Good evening," he offered. More silence. Hard stares. "I couldn't help but hear some of your conversation. May I join you? I'm here alone tonight, which is unusual for me."

They looked at each other. The one who had a bench to himself suddenly slid over, gathering dishes toward him, smiled at Gibb and said, "Sure."

Gibb brought his drink and table setting from the next booth, and sat down. The two opposite him never took their eyes off his face. They had stopped drinking and eating and talking. "What're you guys up to?" he asked. "Sounded interesting."

"'Who are you?' is the question," one said in a sharp tone.

"Oh, a broken-down schoolteacher, collector of tales, novelist, observer of the human scene."

"Yeah? Let's see your FBI/CIA/ABC I.D.," one growled. Then he grinned. They all suddenly relaxed and laughed.

"We know you. We've heard you lecture. You write those crazy stories. That weird shit."

"Flattery will get you anything in my power," Gibb said. They all laughed uproariously, then exchanged names and handshakes, half-standing across the table.

When they settled back, one asked Gibb, "You ever heard of EMP?"

"Sure have," he said. "Electro-magnetic pulse."

"What do you know about it?"

"I understand that one small hydrogen bomb exploded five miles above Omaha will short out every computer in the country except perhaps Key West and Bangor. That if the Soviets have twenty thousand nuclear warheads, it amounts to 19,999 more than they need to bring this civilization to total ruin. That the USSR is less vulnerable, because less dependent on the computer, but becoming more vulnerable every day. That we don't need to threaten to destroy all living things in order to have what those maniacs call "an effective deterrent." That Iran, or Honduras, with one airplane and one bomb, which they can buy from Israel, could do it to this proud country. That one single madman millionaire, of which some exist, could do it to anyone."

"You do know what EMP is. Well, we have a small-scale better idea. Not the whole damn country at once. And no need to sacrifice the good people of Omaha."

Gibb was on his high horse and missed the fact that they were onto something new. He ranted on. "It wouldn't make Omaha much more radioactive than we've already made Hanford and Denver and Cincinnati and Savannah and our own Duke City!"

"You planning to swipe an atomic bomb and a jet airplane?" one asked.

"No." He realized then that they were ready to tell him about their idea and that he was delaying them. "I'm sorry," he said. "I get all lathered up about the waste and the mean-heartedness and the overkill and the real danger to the Biosphere itself."

"Yeah, we noticed."

"So what're you guys gonna put on a flatbed?"

"Clyde's invented, or improved, let's say, a giant magnetic dynamo. His improvement is the miniaturization of it. About the size of a refrigerator. Hooking two together produces ten times the output. We're thinking of hooking four together, which should be about a thousand times. Put 'em on Manny's flatbed. Paint 'em army colors. Drive it downtown. We think it'll short out the computer info, erase the data and the software, within a certain range, so many yards, whatever, maybe as much as a mile. A circle with a mile radius -- that's a lot of data."

"Downtown."

"Yeah. The Electric Power Monopoly first. And then all those banks and the courthouse, and then the phone company. Maybe that'll mess up the phone connections themselves, as well as the records."

"What're you guys mad at?"

"Bigness."

"Drive over by the base, then. Who knows what nasty secret disinformation crap we could erase?"

"Then up to Santa Fe. An experiment results. A large state, with a small population, with no government and no public utilities and no banks. Should be fun."

"Edward Abbey would be proud," Gibb said. "The new Monkey Wrench Gang."

"Lay low a while, then move on to another state. New York and Washington would be the last stops on the tour."

"You guys intend to take over?" Gibb was serious. "Hell, no. That's the point. We don't want anybody taking over anything. We're gonna stop the taking-over process!"

"Aha! Text-book examples, you are -- anarchists!"

"That's probably a good word for us," one said, and they all laughed.

* * *

That night Gibb sat up late, staring at the fire. The city was allowing the use of fireplaces that evening, and he was glad, because staring at a fire helped him think, and he needed to think. But he was remembering, not thinking, unless remembering is a form of thinking. Come to think of it, I guess it is, he thought, grinning to himself.

He was remembering twenty years ago, in their dirty, littered, noisy, stray-dog infested neighborhood -- waking up one summer night to extremely loud music. Not a mariachi party they sometimes were unavoidably let in on in those days, and not the throbbing moveable earthquakes they've had to put up with recently. Real music. Violins, melody, recorded good music, but LOUD. He got up and identified the source of the sound -- a pick-up parked in front of the house across the road. Blasting away Muzak-type, dental-office-memorial, sweet saccharine music! A call to the sheriff's office brought a patrol car quite quickly, and the pick-up drove off.

Next night they were awakened by a loudspeaker, announcing in a pleasant tone, but extremely loudly, "IT'S NOW THREE TWENTY A.M. THAT WAS

MONTOVANI, PLAYING SEVERAL TUNES BY COLE PORTER. NOW THIS FROM THE LOCAL BOTTLERS OF COCA COLA --" The pick-up was parked across the road again. The radio was blasting -- at commercial time. He called the police again and they came again, and the truck drove off.

It happened every night for a week. Every night he called the police. The last night's call was different. "I call every night. They're 'disturbing the peace,' as you phrase it. When the policeman comes, they drive away. Can you not ARREST him, confiscate his truck, or at least his radio? He breaks the law with it every night. Can't you make him turn it OFF, and leave it the hell off?"

The answers to his more and more desperate questions were not at all satisfactory. He continued. "I could turn that radio off. I could go over there with my shotgun and blow that radio away! But you wouldn't like it, if I did that, would you?"

"Oh, no, Sir! Don't do that! We'll get an officer over there right away."

"That's no longer good enough. What gives that guy the right to waken us every night, so that we have to call you?"

"Don't go over there, Sir! I'm sending an officer right now."

And once again, the patrol car came, and the pick-up drove away.

Next day, late in the afternoon, he couldn't get to his own driveway. Police cars, fire trucks, ambulances, TV news teams, a total road block, half a block away. But all the action's at OUR house, he thought, as he approached on foot. No, it's across the street. "What's going on?"

A TV reporter/lady was using their phone to call in her report, so they heard it. "Cases of rifles. Dynamite. Boxes of dynamite. Old. Perhaps sensitive. Police and fire officials are very spooked by it. Special demolition crew is coming. They plan to haul it very carefully south of town and blow it up. Very sensitive -- to physical jolt or even a sudden loud noise. Boxes and boxes of Maoist literature. Revolutionaries. Sabotage."

Gibb imagined his shotgun blast obliterating the radio, and then a ton of ancient Chinese dynamite obliterating houses and revolutionaries and himself and his family and his neighbors and all the stray dogs in that end of town. The family had a good laugh, but it was a little forced on Gibb's part. "Maoists!" he yelped. "Imposters! Daddy Mao would have instructed his followers to turn off the goddam radio!"

* * *

He stared at the fire and thought of his three new revolutionary friends. I guess by knowing about it and not telling Crimestoppers, I'm in on it. A conspiracy to erase data. A conspiracy to turn down Manny's radio and turn up a mini-EMP. Well, so be it.

A bill from the Electric Monopoly which says Gibb owes $400,000.00 for last month's electricity. A receipt from the mortgage company which says his mortgage is paid off. A bank statement which says his balance is $2.1 million.

Any society which lets itself become this vulnerable, while creating such huge numbers of desperately unhappy people is asking to be changed, and deserves whatever happens, he mused. It'll be interesting to watch as it unfolds.

Some Alternative Information Sources:

MAGAZINES

FACTSHEET FIVE, Mike Gunderloy, 6 Arizona Avenue, Rensselaer, NY 12144-4502. Single issue $3.00. Six issue subscription $16. Every two months this reviews, briefly, all of the small press and underground magazines, books, recordings and miscellany that they find out about. A tremendous resource. Everything from the ultra-right to the ultra-left to ultra-sex to comics, the incomprehensibly esoteric, and the just plain weird. A good starting point for freeing yourself from the U.S. propaganda machine and for making new friends.

IDEAS AND ACTION, P.O. Box 40400, San Francisco, CA 94140. Single issue $2.00, four issue subscription $7.50. The magazine for working people creating an anarchist society without bosses or bureaucrats. Topics include labor issues, the environment, women's issues, and international news. Put out three times a year by Workers Solidarity Alliance, the U.S. section of the International Workers Association, the anarchist international.

ANARCHY, c/o C.A.L., P.O. Box 1446, Columbia, MO 65205-1446. Single issue $2.00, six issue subscription $8.00. Every three months Anarchy brings you alternative news, reviews, lists of contacts, and essays that explore the limits of authority and autonomy in our world. Topics include sexuality, ecology, and of course, anarchy. Lots of great graphics.

FIFTH ESTATE, P.O. Box 02548, Detroit, MI 48202. Single issue, $2.00, three issue subscription, $5.00. An anti-technology, primitivist journal that consistently challenges the preconceptions people have about the nature of our civilization. Always interesting.

EARTH FIRST! JOURNAL, P.O. Box 7, Canton, NY 13617. Single issues are $3.00, one year's subscription is $20. Truly radical environmental journal. For those who prefer to save the environment rather than just talking about it or praying to slimeball politicians. No Compromise in the Defense of Mother Earth!

INDUSTRIAL WORKER, IW Collective, 400 W. Washington #2B, Ann Arbor, MI 48103. $2.00 for 6 month subscription. Put out by the Wobblies, (Industrial Workers of the World) America's oldest radical union, still young and still upsetting bosses. Organizes inside and outside of traditional areas, for instance with environmental workers, child care workers, prisoners, and prostitutes.

HOMOCORE, c/o World Power Systems, P.O. Box 77731, San Francisco, CA 94107. Send $1.00 cash only. "Fuck Sexual Conformity". Whether you are hetero or gay or off the scale.

PROCESSED WORLD, 41 Sutter St. #1829, San Francisco, CA 94104. Single issue $3.50. Consistently funny satire and social commentary, often about office workers, computer programmers, etc. Learn about how Amerika runs from people who see it as peons working in the centers of power and greed.

There are lots more, we can't list them all here, check out Factsheet Five!

BOOKS (mail order):

LEFT BANK DISTRIBUTION, 4142 Brooklyn N.E., Seattle, WA 98105. A complete catalog of anarchist literature.

REDWING BLACKBIRD DISTRIBUTION, POB 2042, Decatur, GA 30031-2042. Anarchist periodicals and books.

FLATLAND, POB 2420, Fort Bragg, CA 95437-2420. An interesting selection, mostly fiction, from smaller publishers.

POPULAR REALITY, POB Box 571, Greenwood Lake, NY 10925. Books from the edge, subgenius revoltees, and chaos.

AMOK, P.O. Box 861867, Los Angeles, CA 90086. Have you ever wondered if maybe, somewhere, a few men are controlling everything going on in the world? A catalog of books about paranoia, conspiracy theory, truth posing as fiction, and good unclean fun.

LOOMPANICS, P.O. Box 1197, Port Townsend, WA 98368. A catalog appealing to individualist and right wing anarchists, with useful information for all: weapons, tactics, finances, technology, fake i.d. and tax avoidance, and lots more.

AMADOR PUBLISHERS

The following books are available from Amador Publishers, P.O. Box 12335, Albuquerque, NM 87195. They are 5 1/2 x 8 1/2" paperbacks. Prepaid orders are sent postpaid (NM residents add 5.75% sales tax). Or write Amador for their catalog. Please do not order these books through III Publishing.

THE HUMMINGBIRD BRIGADE by David L. Condit. A counselor's sensitivity to the suffering of others combines with a poet's love of language to soften the barbs of brilliant satire which permeate the novel. $8.00

CROSSWINDS by Michael A. Thomas. A darkly comic modern western in which a young New Mexican with low impulse control struggles to be a sane hardworking citizen. $8.00

CAESAR OF SANTA FE by Tim MacCurdy. A rousing tale of illicit love, describing the administration of Governor Luis de Rosas in Colonial New Mexico around 1640. $9.00

A WORLD FOR THE MEEK by Harry Willson. A post-blast fantasy in which the lone survivor finds love and meaning among the dolphins and the octopi. $9.00

TAIL TIGERSWALLOW AND THE GREAT TOBACCO WAR by Arthur L. Hoffman. Glenn Morgan's personal vendetta against the cigarette companies carries him from Chicago to the Albuquerque Balloon Fiesta, and ranges from simple sabotage to outright guerrilla warfare. $8.00

Books by Amador Publishers (Cont.)

SOULS AND CELLS REMEMBER by Harry Willson. A tender love story full of anger and ancient longings, cultural confrontation and reincarnation, moving from New Mexico to the Susquehanna and in time from the present to the 1750's. $8.00

THE CARLOS CHADWICK MYSTERY by Gene H. Bell-Villada. How and why does a college kid become a radical, possibly a terrorist? This college romance political satire furnishes an in-depth portrait of today's American mind. $9.00

DUKE CITY TALES by Harry Willson. "Duke City" is Albuquerque, complete with luminarias, balloons, atomic bombs, DWI, cops and a fumbling old alchemist. $8.00

EVA'S WAR by Eva Krutein. A gripping, true story of gripping story of flight, refugees, privation, defeat, moral quandaries, and finally healing through music in Danzig in 1945. $9.00

TWELVE GIFTS: RECIPES FROM A SOUTHWEST KITCHEN by Adela Amador. $3.00.

If you like satire you'll love:

THE LAST DAYS OF CHRIST THE VAMPIRE

by J.G. Eccarius

He rose from the dead ...

His power grew over the ages. Enslaving minds and bodies through religious hierarchies and direct telepathic control, Jesus Christ promised people eternal life in return for obedience.

Professor Holbach thinks Christ the Vampire is just a metaphor giving him nightmares. But when he starts telling his story to others he and his friends are attacked and must flee for their lives. This is the story of how they fight back against this ancient horror.

"One of the most wildly blasphemous books we have seen since the classics of sacrilege."
 - Fifth Estate

"A book of stunning originality, full of surrealistic shocks and haunting images."
 - Robert Anton Wilson

"Iconoclasm at its most engaging ... be forewarned, you'll never want to take holy communion again!"
 - Small Press Review

"Takes the vampire theme for a ride on a new roller coaster ... fun, entertaining, and in a few places hilarious."
 - L. Chernyi in Anarchy

"Bizarre."
 - Locus

ISBN 0-9622937-0-9
184 pages, paperback

$6.00 from III Publishing

Also from III Publishing:

WE SHOULD HAVE KILLED THE KING

by J.G. Eccarius

"Eccarius is back with another novel that is even more eccentric than the first. It concerns the life and times of Jack Straw, anarcho-communist, para-legal, bohemian and eventually elder. The book jumps around from a constrained childhood to an anarchist future fantasy which starts out with a hopeful enclave and ends with a sunburned dead world, (thanks to CFC's). Along the way Eccarius casts his light on a few features of the modern political scene, from the WPPSS debacle to Autonomen fighting in the streets in Germany. His characterization of the RCP is particularly cutting. All in all, an interesting, chewy, different book."

-Factsheet Five

192 pages, paperback, $5.00

To order: send cash, check or money order (made out to III Publishing) to III Publishing, P.O. Box 170363, San Francisco, CA 94117-0363. Or request a free catalog.

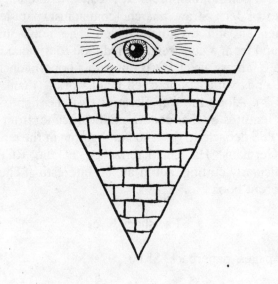